Run to New York

Victoria Cole

Copyright © 2024 by Victoria Cole

All rights reserved.

No portion of this book may be reproduced in any form without written permission from the publisher or author, except as permitted by U.S. copyright law.

CONTENTS

CHAPTER 1

S he does a turn and then slides down to the floor into a split, as the song continues to play she moves her body to the music gracefully and ends her solo with her walking away. The Judges tally up the scores and pass it to the Host, and the winner is... drum rolls went off. Kimberley the Host announces, but as she is accepting the trophy for her wonderful ballet performance, her name kept rolling out of the Host mouth like a broken record and she pulls out of her dream by her father who is calling her the entire time.

"Dad?" she groans but her father places his finger to his lips to tell her to be quiet.

"Someone is in the house," he says and as she listens, she could hear the voices of unknown men moving around downstairs.

"What are we going to do and where is David?" asks Kim.

"In his room under his bed, go get him and do what I taught you if something like this were to happen, remember

Kimberley run as far as you can and do not look back." Kim nods at her father's words and bolts quickly but quietly to her brother's room.

As Kim enters her brother's room she calls out for him in the dark and when he appears, she says to him, "Come out we have to run while dad distracts them."

David being the clumsy little boy he is accidentally hits the stand next to the closet causing loud noise to erupt in the room and no later than two seconds heavy footsteps start making its way upstairs. Bam, Bam, two shots rang in the air followed by men shouting.

Kimberley grabs her brother and goes into the closet that he came out of hiding from and heads to the back behind the clothes. "Stay here and whatever you do, do not move you got it," she tells David as she holds him by the shoulders.

David grabs her hand to pull her back, with tears falling from his eyes he whispers "Am scared KJ."

Kimberley looks at her brother and replies, "I know DJ but you have to be brave," while she continues to stare at him an idea suddenly came into her mind and she goes into the room, grabs the tablet and headphones to give to him so he can be distracted.

Kim makes her way to the wall where a painting of a Beach-front is hanging and removes it. Since David and Kimberley's room is next to each other there is a small hole in the wall to watch David when she had too much homework and had to burn the midnight oil on her college courses. Looking through it she could not help but gasp at what is happening on the other side of the wall. Her father is kneeling down bloodied to the point where one of his eyes could not open.

"Where is it?" one of the men asks.

"Where is what?" her father replies, he goes on to say "It can be many things such as a boat, car, food, money or it can even be a card to a good plastic Surgeon, one that you desperately need because let me tell you, buddy, I thought you were wearing a mask, I did not know that was your natural look."

The men look at him and laugh, then all of a sudden a punch is thrown his way and Kimberley who is still watching covers her mouth to stop the noise from escaping.

"Now Mr. Jones tell me where is the software that we are looking for?"

Mr. Jones looks at the one questioning him and asks him to come a little bit closer and when the man is close enough, Mr. Jones whispers to him, "Ask your mother, I left my belongings thereafter our midnight night snack," then he ends his sentence with a wink.

In so much rage the man pulls out his gun and points it to Mr. Jones's head.

"Search the house, rip it apart if you have to, anything you find electronically take it to the car he orders the men around." With the gun still position to Mr. Jones's head, the man continues,   "And as for you Mr. Jones, good riddance," Bam! the gun goes off killing Mr. Jones.

Tears fall down her face as she watches her father die mercilessly by the hands of those horrendous men. Kim makes her way to the Closet and pulls apart the clothes that are behind her brother. Pushing back the wall it reveals a secret passage that looks dark and dusty at the entrance.

Grabbing her brother who is asleep, she makes her way down the dark hallway which will take her into the woods. When she arrives at her destination she pushes the wooden door open and runs as fast as she can holding her little brother tightly to her chest and not long after, an explosion happens from behind them. Kim watches as her childhood home goes up in flames.

There is more to come so stay tune chapter 2 will be here shortly!!!!!

CHAPTER 2

Sitting up in the Cabin dirty and confuse is not how Kimberley pictured life at eighteen would be. She thought she would finally break out of her shell and try new things, but now she is sitting on the sofa thinking about the terrifying night she has had. From waking up to burglar to watching her father get shot between the eyes, it is too much for her to take in and now she is stuck with her eight-year-old brother on her hands.

As she gets up she looks around the cabin remembering that it is her father secret hideout. Every year since her mom died she would have a drill course about how to find the hideout if a situation like this would occur and now she wonders what secrets her father kept from her.

As she is heating the hot water for hot chocolate and soup for her and her brother, David comes out of the room rubbing the sleep out of his eyes.

"KJ where is Daddy?" he asks causing Kim to look at her little brother with teary eyes and then she makes her way to him.

"Remember when I told you mom went to Heaven to be an Angel, well our Daddy went there also so that he could protect us until we are ready to go," she replies.

"I miss him already," says David.

"Me too," Kimberley replies.

"Hey, am whipping up some food for us to eat, would you like to watch TV?" Kimberley says as she bends down to his level, she is doing everything she can to keep his mind off the situation because in her mind David is too young to be put into situations like this, so they make their way over to the living room.

Next to the television is a tiny shelf that is filled with DVD's and as Kim is about to put a DVD inside the player, she notices a DVD already inside of it. Taking it out it reads, to Kim from Dad, so she decides to play it and on the screen is her father.

"Kim if you are watching this it means am already with your mother eating chicken breast and drinking red wine or in my case apple cider because we all know no alcohol is allowed at the front gates to be let into heaven, I should know I tried to sneak one in before but the Angels threw me back down to earth." Kim laughs because even in death her father always kept his sense of humor going.

"Now listen attentively Kim", at this she sits up straight on the sofa, "I have created something that can change technology as we know it but it can also be a deadly weapon to people who have bad intentions, now what I need you to do is gather everything you and your Brother own and head to New York City where you will find clues to where I hid it. Whatever you do cover your tracks because they are after the software I created when this video is finished destroy this along with the Cabin."

Meanwhile, the men are reporting back to their Boss on their findings and what transpired.

"What should we do now? We have no one to lead us to the Software because instead of worrying about locating it, you killed the creator."

"Not entirely true Mr. Valentino, says Stephen a computer literate."

"Explain?" says the boss as he crosses his arms and waits for Stephen to talk.

"Well I have been doing some digging and I found that Mr. Jones has two children, a girl, and a boy to be exact," says Stephen as he pushes his glasses up on his nose feeling proud of himself.

"Interesting, I want names and any other information you can pull up?" Mr. Valentino says standing up from his seat.

"Already have them, Kimberley Jones just turn eighteen graduated High school at the age of fifteen during that time in school she was starting college classes where her majors were computer engineering and software engineering, she just receive her Bachelor's degree and David Jones age eight haven't started school as yet because he has a low immune system and gets sick easily, his father thought keeping him home would be in his best interest."

"Are there any photos of them?" Valentino asks as he walks up to Stephen.

"Yes sir, here they are."

As the photos are pass to Valentino he could not help but gasp because the beautiful girl in the picture was the girl who saves him when he was left for dead in an alleyway five years ago, she might have been thirteen but he remembers that day clearly.

Flashback

Mr. Valentino was meeting up with his clients when one of them pulled a gun and shot him, he was appalled that someone went against him and tried to take him out and just as he was about to slip into unconsciousness, a little Angel appeared saying stay with me you are going to be okay. Two weeks later he woke up with her tending to him, she had community service at the Hospital and by the time he was released, she had already completed her hours.

He never forgot her and she was too young to have a relationship with, but now that she is old enough he will be taking her as his bride.

"Kill two birds with one stone," he says, then goes on and orders his men to, "locate the Software and capture Kim to become his wife."

Laughing out loud he begins to think, "Mr. Jones should have never played him because his death could have been prevented and his daughter could have had a father to walk her down the Isles."

Going to the door he says, "Stephen knowing Jones he might have own Cabins find it and you find the girl, tell my men to bring her to me unharmed and untouched."

As Kimberley drive to the Airport, she keeps looking in the rearview mirror to see if anyone is trailing behind her because she knows it is a matter of time before they figure out about her and David, especially if they have Stephen working on their team. She knows about Stephen because her Dad mentioned it in the video that he left behind. Parking the car she goes to check her and David in, then sits down in the waiting area.

Thinking back on how her Dad used to talk about Stephen and how he a prodigy in the computer world but it all ended when her Dad comes home saying he has cause danger to come upon his family, that is when her Dad started to pay more attention to work forgetting that home is where he should have been.

Taking a seat on the plane she lays her head back and smiles because she knows it is a matter of time before they saw the little present she left them.

"Valentino I find a Cabin that Mr. Jones owns before his wife died they would go there, the men are heading up that way now!" one of the men says.

"Excellent!" replies Valentino as he hangs up, then he turns to Stephen and continues, "soon my fiancé you will be mine."

Rolling his eyes, Stephen continues on his laptop only to realize something is wrong.

"What in the Buddha shrine is happening, oh no, no, no, no, no!" Stephen grabs his phone and calls Valentino's men, "Get out of there, it's a trap, run now." Not long after an explosion interrupts his ranting.

"Talk to me what is happening?" asks Valentino.

"Kimberley is as trickery as her Dad and did I mention wise, it seems the door had a trap her father set at the house that when the men enter, the door shuts and the wire connecting to the explosives will go off and she left something on my laptop after hacking it."

Showing Valentino the laptop, it reads:

WE HIDE YOU SEEK! GAME ON BASTARDS!

xoxo, YOUR PAIN IN THE BEHIND!

Valentino sits there looking at the laptop and grinning like a Cheshire Cat and says game on my girl, game on.

CHAPTER 3

Sitting on the sofa in her Apartment, a year has passed since the night her father was murdered. Kim is on her laptop looking at her brother's recent pictures that she took when he joined the little league's softball team when suddenly her phone rings. "Hello" she answers and in response, the person is asking "Is this Ms. Kimberley Jones?"

Confuse she takes the phone from her ear, looks at it then says, "This is she," and the person tells her she has an interview with the CEO of Diaz Incorporation in the morning at 8 am sharp and the call ends immediately.

When she hangs up, she can not contain her excitement and is jumping up and down on the sofa because this is the moment she waited on.

"What happen KJ?" asks David and with a squeal, she replies telling him that she is being interviewed tomorrow and if she gets the job then it will mean that more income will come to them. After hearing what his sister says, he too jumps up on the sofa with excitement.

A few seconds after their excitement dies down, a knock appears at the door making Kim get up to go get it. Thinking it's the pizza delivery guy, she opens it and standing in front of her is a tall man dress in all black with tattoo's running up and down his arm.

"Well if it isn't Kimberley," says the man with a sinister smirk but before he can finish she gasps and slams the door in his face.

"David I need you to go hide for me and do not come out unless I tell you to", Kimberley tells David causing him run-up to the room

Upon hearing banging on the door, Kim runs to the phone to call the police when the door bursts open causing a scream to escape her mouth and the man comes in with anger in his eyes. "You think you can escape Valentino after that stunt you pulled in Australia? Well, you can't, I am going to drag you back by the hair if I have to," he says loudly.

"You are Valentino's property, now, be a good girl and come with me," he says as he slowly starts to approach her. Even though fear is in Kim's body, she puts on a brave face, straightens her back and tells him, "No."

"What?" he replies with venom on his lips then takes deep breaths with his eyes closes.

Kim starts to back away and when he notices that he begins to talk, "You know if your father had given the software that Valentino invested in none of this would have happened but because of your humanitarian act six years ago, it proves you to be an eligible bride for him."

"Others just like me are running around looking for you but do not worry, he does not know where you are because it is my lead that causes me to find you. My little brother died in that explosion you created at the Cabin and now am going to make your life a living hell." With that, he launches at Kim and wraps his hands around her neck choking her to death.

With all the strength she has left, Kim raises her right knee and sends it into his private part causing him to collapse on the floor while he groans and holds his area. Coughing whiles trying to take in as much oxygen as possible, Kim made her way to the kitchen to retrieve the other phone but before she can make a call, she is knocked to the ground and turn over.

The guy begins choking her again, but this time he is adding more pressure and Kim is trying to pull his hands away while kicking her feet. Her vision is starting to get blurry and as she is about to close her eyes completely, she feels hot liquid on her face causing her eyes to snap open as she feels the pressure removing from her neck.

Looking around, she takes in the scene that is playing out in front of her then gasp in horror. Her little brother is holding a knife that he uses to stab the man with causing the man to turn around and say, "You are a dead kid," and starts to make his way to him.

Kim could not watch this man murder her little brother that she swore to protect, without thinking she grabs one of the butcher knives, runs behind the man and stabs him in the head. The man drops to the floor and when Kim discovers what she has done, she screams then passes out.

Although being too young to understand anything, David is wise beyond his years and when he hears the man downstairs yelling at his sister, he quietly makes his way to where his sister is. As he enters the living room, he comes across an empty room with his sister's cell phone on the ground and decides it would be best to call the police but stops when he hears noise from the kitchen.

Dropping the phone, he quickly enters the kitchen where he found his sister underneath the man being choked to death. Climbing on the stool, he grabs a knife then he jumps onto the man back and plunges the knife there.

When the man releases his sister to come after him, he becomes frightened but remains still thinking he did what he did to protect the only family he has left. After the man collapsed with a knife stuck in his head and the horrifying scream of his sister, he runs out the door to get help and thankfully everyone on that floor helps him.

CHAPTER 4

Waking up in a dark room causes Kim to panic, until she sees her brother curl up on the seat next to her. Looking around the room, she sees a bag in the corner and gets up to look inside of it where she finds her personal belongings.

The door opens and in walks Dr. Michaelson who treated her when she was emitted in the hospital. "I see you are awake, how are you feeling?" asks Dr. Michaelson. She replies by saying "I feel like I was thrown out of a three story window but I guess being choke to death can do that to you."

Dr. Michaelson laughs, "I guess I should give you a checkup and discharge you."

Smiling at what he says, Kim nods and looks at her phone to see that it is 6:30 am. "That will be great, I have an interview at 8:00 so the earlier I get out of here the better."

As she makes her way out of the hospital carrying her brother who is still asleep, her friend is waves at her to show her she is there. She places her brother in the backseat and jumps in the passenger seat.

"Thank you so much Melissa for getting my stuff and bringing it to the hospital, also for keeping an eye on my brother," she says as she buckles up.

" Melissa smiles and says, "Look I know you and I use to talk on the computer before you moved here and I know about what happened back in Australia that made you run here, but what if this guy sends more people here to hurt you, am worried about you, I mean have you look in the mirror at your face and neck? If he were to get away, the police can identify him from the imprints."

Kim takes a deep breath and says, "You are right but I need to get home to take a shower, and get to my interview, I need something to take my mind off just killing someone she chokes out."

Melissa hugs Kim tightly, there is worry in her voice as she says, "How about we go to my place and from there you can find another place to move into. I do not feel comfortable with you going back there after last night." Kim nods her head agreeing.

Applying make up and tying a scarf around her neck, Kim tries to make her bruises less visible for her interview. Making her way out she goes to check on her brother to see if he is alright.

"Hey BJ I came here to check on you." She says in a soft voice as she rubs his back.

"Am okay KJ, it's you am worried about and am scared that you will end up like daddy," he say as he sniffles a little.

Hearing those words come out of his mouth made tears well up in her eyes because her brother is too young to have seen those kind of things happen.

"I got to head out for my interview and you have to go to school so lets get going," she says trying to brighten his mood.

Kim drops her brother to school and makes her way to the coffee shop next to Diaz Incorporation. Her interview starts at 8:00 but it is only 7:40, so she decides it will be best to get energize for her interview. Walking in she gets her coffee and donut she orders, then walks to the door where she runs into a person causing her coffee to spill all over their suit.

"Am so sorry, I can..." but before she can finish her sentence, the man speaks to her in a harsh voice and asks, "Are you blind? Do you know how much this suit cost?"

Kim could not believe her ears, this man have the audacity to speak to her like this and she is not going to be talk to bad by a rude man in a expensive suit, so she speaks just as rude as him.

"Did you not hear me apologizing? Next time when you see someone walking your way go around and maybe an accident can be avoided."

The man clenches his teeth and says, "Excuse you, know your place women, he went on to talk to her but Kim interrupts him raising her voice saying, "NO! you know your place and act like someone teach you some damn manners," and ends it with smashing the donut in his face and walking out.

Kim walks into Diaz Incorporation mad because she could not believe what stick was stuck up that mans butt to insult her like that. Making her way to the receptionist she tells them she is here for the interview.

The receptionist assists her to go the 40th floor and tells her Mr. Diaz is waiting for her. As Kim takes the elevator to the 40th floor her mind wonder back on last night events and it felt like she could not breathe all over again. Taking deep breaths the door finally opens showing nothing but pure chaos. People are running everywhere and in the background you can hear a man shouting.

Kim goes close to the door that says, "Mr. Alexander Diaz CEO" and upon entering there is men standing in suits being yell at because apparently the boss has a 9:00 meeting and no one can find the files that is store on the computer.

Kim ignores the boss and walks past everyone to the computer that is sitting on the desk and starts to look for the missing files.

"What the hell are you doing here and why are you on my computer?" Kim holds up her finger telling him to wait one moment and the voice shouts call security up here now.

About three seconds later Kim says, "found it! Apparently someone deleted the files but before they did, they made a copy whereas it was hidden in a new folder.

When Kim looks up, her eyes falls upon stone cold eyes and a familiar face. Swallowing hard she says, "My name is Kimberley Jones and I am here for my interview with Mr. Diaz."

The man replies, "I am Mr. Diaz and you can leave because the interview would not be happening, how do I know you did not delete the files and came back to impress me? You could be a spy for another company, so let the security escort you out.

Anger runs through Kim's veins at what this man just imply. "Are you serious? You know what forget you and this interview I can walk myself out."

With tears rolling down her face as she walks out of Diaz Incorporation, Kim makes her way down the sidewalk of New York City thinking about how the opportunity of a lifetime slip away. She approaches a park and sits on the bench crying. No later than five minutes she hears someone yelling stop him.

Her head follows the voice and notice a man carrying a woman purse as he looks to be running away. Kim gets up and tackles him as he tries to run past her but the man rolls them over and punches Kim in the face.

Even thought the punch hurt because of her previous injuries, that did not stop Kim from jumping on his back, strangling him, and biting his shoulder. The man yells and flips her over causing her to land on her back, then he kicks her.

As he is going to give Kim another kick, the man stops and panic because he hears the sirens of a Police vehicle. Escaping, he leaves the purse and Kim on the ground.

"Oh my Lord a women appears and bends down next to Kim asking her to stay awake, help is on the way." Kim grabs the purse handing it to the women and says, "I am okay, I hate people who pray upon vulnerable women," then she passes out.

CHAPTER 5

Waking up in a hospital bed feels like deja vu for Kim, but his time she isn't alone. Melissa is sitting on a chair with David on her lap and an unknown woman is in another chair. Sitting up Kim starts moaning at the pain she is feeling in her back, face and stomach.

Upon hearing her moan Melissa jumps up out of the seat and begins ranting about how she needs to take it easy and she will look for the doctor.

"Glad to see you are awake" a soft voice says from the other seat, causing Kim to turn her head and face the women who she help earlier.

"Yes I am awake, thanks for staying but you did not have to," Kim says.

"Am good, just a little shook by the turn of events, my name is Kerry but enough about me Kim, Melissa has told so much about you."

"Kerry as in Melissa's Aunt?" Kim asks as she turns her head to the side.

Smiling, Kerry winks and says, "The one and only," then she grabs Kim's hands and asks "Do you have anyone I can call for you?" Kerry asks.

Kim replies, "No! both my mother and father are decease, so I decided to move here from Australia with my little brother."

"Wow you are such a responsible young lady especially at this age," Kerry says as she rubs her shoulder.

Kim smiles and says in a shy voice "Thank you."

The doors open and in walks Dr. Michaelson, "we meet again Kim if you keep getting hurt like this every time, people are going to start thinking this is your excuse to see me," he says with a cheesy smile on his face.

Kim laughs at Dr. Michaelson and says as she rolls her eyes, "Yea because getting a concussion have me falling hard for you." Everyone in the room starts laughing including David who has just awake.

"Kerry!" Someone bursts through the doors shouting, then asks, "Are you okay honey?"

"Calm down Charles, am alright, better than the women that save me," Kerry answers as she looks at the man with adoration.

Charles took a deep breath and turns to look at Kim. "Thank you!" he says to her and Kim holds up her hands and replies, "No problem, I would like to think someone will do it for me if I was in that situation." Charles smiles and gives her a nod of approval.

"Mother," more voices comes at the door but one voice stands out and it is the devil himself, Alexander Diaz. As he walks in, Alexander looks at Kim and she looks back wondering how she can not notice the resemblance in him and his father.

Dr. Michaelson begins to speak, "Well Kim, looks like you not only have two broken ribs but a slight concussion as well as bruises with swelling that line up and down your spine. Thank God that man did not do more damage because you would have end up in a coma or worst."

From the corner David starts to cry and runs to Kim. "KJ you could have gone to Heaven just like daddy, please KJ be careful."

"It's okay buddy I was only helping someone who needed help, but next time I will try to find a two by four and swing," she says as she rubs his head.

David pouts and says, "KJ you really trying to give me a heart attack, am getting too old for this. At this everyone starts to laugh in the room.

"By the way KJ, did you get the Job? Did the interview went well?" he asks then shakes his head and says, "No wait, I know you did because Sissy always does good." David says grinning.

Kim replies to David telling him she did not get the Job causing David to frown and say, "Oh am sorry Sissy" in a sad voice. A second later, he puts on a serious face and says, "Don't you worry, you will find another one, I know you will because as daddy always use to say, we Jones are, are, are...

Knowing what he wants to say, Kim finishes his sentence by saying, "Tenacious."

"That's right!" David says and Kim laughs at him and bring him in for a hug where she discovers he is burning up severely.

"David did you take your medication? You are burning up," she says in panic.

David looks, down and mumbles a "no" but Kim hears him.

"David why?" she asks sternly as she awaits his answer.

Tucking his lips in, he looks up at Kim with tears in his eyes then says, "Because I did not want the medication to empty quickly, we were low on income and knowing that you were waiting on being hire at Diaz Incorporation, I wanted to wait until you have that Job so we can be financially stable and then I can take my meds everyday."

Kim huffs and with tears in her eyes says, "David I do not mind the medication running out because I will always be able to afford it. Especially when it comes up to your well being, so please take it everyday or I will tickle you everyday for the rest of your life."

Looking at David, she sees that he still is sad and to cheer him up she smirks then says, "Even when you are old enough start dating, I will tickle you in front of your girlfriend," then she starts to tickle him. Laughs from both Kim and David has everyone in the room smiling at them.

Kim forgets that she is not alone and hangs down her head in embarrassment. "Sorry I forget that you all were still here."

"It's okay, you are a very wise young adult and David is a very smart boy for his age, Kerry says as she looks at them with joy in her eyes.

Melissa looks at her friend, "You know you could have ask me for help right?"

Kim replies by saying, "Yes, but I like doing things on my own and I do not like bothering people with my situations.

Melissa shakes her head, "I would not mind you are my friend."

Alexander who is watching from the corner of the room steps forward, "Ms. Jones my attitude was inappropriate to you and I should not have kicked you out of the company nor accuse you of being a spy."

"You have help me not only make the biggest deal for the company but you have help me find the person responsible for causing information to fall into the wrong hands. I would be greatful to have you join our company."

"Does that mean my Sissy gets the Job?" asks David.

"Yes indeed she does have it if she still wants it," Alexander says as he looks at Kim awaiting her answer.

Kim looks at David and asks, "What do you think buddy?"

"Take it, Take it, Take it," David chants along with everyone in the room.

"Okay I will" Kim agrees with a small chuckle.

Alexander face shows appreciation, "Well since you agree you will be moving into one of the Companies Penthouses and from there we will discuss your working arrangements but first get some rest, your body needs healing," he says.

Kim and Alex keeps staring at each other like they were the only two in the room. Charles decides to speak, "Well now that everything is settle lets get going. Kim, David it is nice meeting the two of you and I hope to see you again soon, get some rest.

As everyone walks out, Alex turns around and gives one last look to Kim and then exits the room. Kim who is still staring at the door couldn't help the feeling she get when Alex looks at her. Her heart skips a beat and as she closes her eyes, her dreams consist of Alexander and his beautiful, stone cold eye.

Chapter 6

It has been four weeks since everything happen and to say it was crazy for Kimberley would be and understatement. Looking out of the window of her Condo is surreal for her because she never thought in her wildest dreams she would be in this stage in her life.

"Sissy Mr. Diaz is here to see you," says David.

Turning around Kimberley looks at Alexander standing there as he leans on the door staring with his gray eyes upon her, causing her to blush.

Can I help you with something Mr. Diaz? she asks as she bites her bottom lip.

Seconds past with him staring at her and when the silence becomes too long, he stands up straight and says, "I came to see if you were settling in your new environment."

"It is nice, but did you have to come here to for that," asks Kim.

Alex starts walking close to her and stops directly in front of her.

"I had to because of my actions..." but Kim cuts him off saying she did not blame him for his actions it was a bad time for him.

Alex looks at her to see her biting her bottom lip and he exhales harshly and places his thumb on her bottom lip and with deep breaths he says, "Stop biting your lip or you would not like the consequences.

Kim blushes and looks down, a thought passes through her mind so she decides to ask, "what convince you that I was not a spy in your company?"

Alexander stare at her for a while before speaking saying that him and his security team watch the footage and saw one of their own walking into his office and after minutes went by he exited.

"When he question him he lied and after we search his place we found files on his computer belonging to the company that was sent to another company, he was the spy in the company."

"Oh that is insane, I can't believe that a person would do that, well actually I could believe because that is the same way how my father was screwed over before he passed. It's just that am sorry you had to go through that." As Kim keeps ranting, Alexander pulls her into a hug and she breathes in his scent.

"Thank you," says Alexander and she replies "You're welcome Mr. Diaz.

"Please call me Alexander," he says and smiles at her.

Kim nods yes and asks, "Can I call you Alex?

He stiffen but later nods his head yes, "See you Monday Kim," and walks out.

Kim went to the front desk to ask about the key card and if it is ready for the entrance and other amenities. Mr. Ronald the guy behind the desk hands her an envelope and goes over a few policies.

Walking back up to her room she sees men dress in all black standing outside the door across from her. A man comes out and is push to the floor by one of the men in black. Afraid for him Kim scolds the man who push the poor man.

Are you alright? Do you need help? she asks as she bends down to his level.

The man on the ground smile and says, "That would be great."

After Kim helps the man she offers to take him to dinner because as she is helping him, she discovers he just lost his job. As they makes their way to the restaurant across the street, Kim looks back to notice one of the men is on the phone.

They goes into the restaurant and sits down. Kim smiles at him and is about to say something but the guy speaks at the same time as her. No you first they both say, No you they both say again and laughs.

"Ladies first," the man says.

Kim replies, "Men were created first so go ahead."

"Too shay my friend," he says then goes on to ask, "So what are you doing living in New York, you sound like you are from England or is it Ireland?

Kim laughs and says, "Actually, I am from Australia and to answer your other question I am a computer nerd along with other things so I have to expand my horizon with my skills."

"So tell me Cam is it short for Camden?" Kim asks.

"Nope it is really short for Camron," he says as he rubs his neck.

"Nice your parents sure had a name discussion before you were born because usually Cam is short for Camden," says Kim as she takes a sip of her drink.

Cam laughs and says, "Yea that's what I loved the most about my parents, they always had their life planned out, even down to what their children would be name."

"So where are they now?" asks Kim who rests her chin in her palm listening to Camron.

Cam mood went down then he replies, "They passed away in a car accident."

"Oh am so sorry for intruding, I know the feeling my mother passed away when my brother and I were young and my father passed away recently," she says sadly.

Cam nods his head in understanding and then asks, "So would you like to come to with me to the new seafood restaurant? You can call it a date."

"Absolutely not" a deep voice says behind Kim.

Kim turns around and is startle to see Alexander standing there with gray angry eyes, dress in black just like the men surrounding him.

Through clench teeth Alexander says, "Camron I thought I told you to leave and never come around anything or anyone who belongs to me."

Camron face turns blue and Kim is confuse so she speaks and asks, "Cam how do Alex know you?" But before anyone can answer, she goes on to say, "Oh this is perfect, Alex, Cam needs a Job he just got layed off from his."

"Kim I don't think that is a good idea, just lets get our food and go." Camron says.   Cam grabs her arm and went to turn around but felt her being pull from his grip.

"You didn't you hear me clearly, you are not taking her any-where with you," Alexander says while wrapping his hands around her. "Not only did you disobey my orders but you messing with what belongs to me," he states.

Anger arise in Cam face as he yells, "She does not belong to you, she is not property and she can make her own decisions."

Alexander pushes Kim into one of his men arms and goes up into Camron's face.

"Kim is mine whether she knows it or not, so get this through your thick skull, stay away from her, she is too innocent to be around someone like you and if I catch you around her, you will wish that you have never been born," spits Alexander with venom.

Alexander grabs Kim and tells Brandon to pay for the food the waitress is holding and bring it to where Kim was staying. As they went into the car Kim asks Alex, "Why did you do that to Camron?" Alex tells her that Camron was the man that was fired for spying on the company.

"That's the guy?" Kim asks. "And here I am asking you to give him a Job, oh how I am having a blonde moment."

Alexander arrives to the Condominiums and escorts Kim to her door. Brandon comes up behind Alex. "Kim meet Brandon, a close buddy of mine," Alex says as he puts he his on Brandon shoulder.

"Yea I saw him when they were throwing Cam out," she says while laughing. There is a long pause before she asks, "Is he the reason to how you know that I was with Cam?"

"Don't say his name ever again and yes he contact me, I do not want Cam close to you because it was a lot more things I found out during my investigation," says Alex with an angry look.

Kim huffs then says, "My father always said being nice is not good because people will take advantage of me, I can't help that I am a magnet for people like them."

"That is why I am going to keep you close to my side" says Alexander, then he kisses her on the forehead. "Goodnight Kim" he hands her the takeout.

Kim replies by saying, "Goodnight" and runs inside. Leaning on the door she can feel her heart beating hard and fast, she places a hand on her chest as she wonders, "Is this what having a crush feels like or is it something else?"

Chapter 7

"**S**itting in my office, I lean back in my chair thinking about the blonde that came into my life. I can't remember ever having this feeling with the other women that passed through my life.

Walking into that Café and having her spill her drink on me, I wanted to send her crying for the hills but the minute my eyes behold her beauty, she gave off a sense telling me she needed protection. Yes, I know she told me some things that was disrespectful and the fire that was in her blue eyes made her look more hot than she was, but you can tell she was innocent with a drop of shyness."

"When she arrived in my office and did what she did, I could not help but think that my competition send a vixen to draw me in and bring down my company. That is why I let her go because I was not going to be played by another woman. But looking at the security camera with my men I discovered the truth that same day, Camron was my most trusted computer genius aside from Jared and when Jared came back that day from his trip, he was the only one I could rely on to do some digging."

That day when I got the call from my Dad telling me what happen, I immediately went to the scene and saw a puddle of blood on the floor. Many people was watching and I know somebody saw something so I decided to ask, offering $100,000 to anyone who had seen what happen."

"A little boy who was at the park skating had heard scream-ing and went to see what had happen, thankfully he got it on video too. When Jared played it on the laptop, to say I was mortified would be an understatement, seeing her being beating like that sent anger through my veins and there was no way in hell I was letting this criminal get away with what he did."

"As Jared dealt with the footage, I made my way to the Hospital. Seeing her like that sent guilt through me, knowing that if I hadn't let her go she would be alright, but then again I would not have seen how caring she is toward people especially strangers."

"I mean come on, what kind of girl throws herself in harms way for a stranger. Listening to her and her little brother I could not help but feel more guilt because she has so much responsibilities by herself, that is why I have to make it right, I am starting to feel something for her even though we just meant but I am willing to not push it."

"Then my mind wonders to Camron, that bastard decided to go out with my girl and made up some bull crap lie about being fired because of some ridiculous reason, knowing full well what he really was fired for, and my little Angel is so sweet, caring and so, so, so, so naïve that she believe everything that he said."

"When my friend called me and told me that she was going with Camron to the restaurant, I had to hurry up and finish my meeting. People thought I was going insane and when I walk into that restaurant, hearing him ask her on a date. That will never happen, she is mine, I need to make sure nobody tries to take her from me and use her because of the way she is."

"A knock came on the door breaking me from my thoughts."

"Mr. Diaz your father is here to see you," my secretary says.

"Let him in," I say and my old man walks through the door.

"Son how you are you doing?"

"Not good Dad, would you believe Camron try to make a move on Kim?" I ask him with anger lacing in my words.

"Well Son, she does capture men attention and her naïve ways or should I say her innocence makes people want to be with or around her, I personally want to protect her because she is still too young to know anything about this world and the people in it, says my Dad with amusement in his eyes.

"I know Dad that is why I raise the security station at the Condo to keep an extra eye on her," I reply to him.

Looking at my Dad I see he is in deep thought, "What is it Dad?"

"Nothing son, she just reminds me of an old friend of mine, his name was Edward Jones but the last time I heard from him is when he sold me some paintings and told me to take care of them." "His wife had some of Kimberley ways and Kim does look like her, where as David looks like a mini version of Edward," my Dad say rubbing his head.

"Well Kim might be related to them in some ways her last name is Jones," I say to my father causing him to go off in thought again."

"Well son your mom wants you at the banquet next month hopefully Kimberley will be on your arm, the sly old fox says getting up.

"Hopefully? Dad Kimberley will be on my arm and as my girl too. With a smile on my face I set my plan into motion."

CHAPTER 8

Waking up Monday morning to the alarm going off, has Kimberley bolting through her place to get ready for work.

"David where are you? It is time for School," she yells.

David is sitting at the counter eating lucky charms while he watches cartoon on his tablet, making Kimberley place her hands on her waist and scold him for wasting his time on the tablet.

After dropping David off to School, she makes her way to work where she is introduce to the friendly staff. Going in the Elevator, she makes her way up to Mr. Diaz office where she encounters yelling by Mr. Diaz himself.

Kimberley groans and under her breath she says, "Not again."

As she stops in front of the door, she is about to knock when the door flies open and a man runs straight into her knocking them both to the ground. Alexander who is sitting down at his desk jumps up and runs to the door. Looking at the scene in front of him makes his blood boil.

Kimberley is on the floor underneath the man and his left hand is gripping her breast, while his mouth is on her cheek. Brandon has just walk out of the Elevator where he takes in the scene in front of him.

"I have walk into many awkward situations in my life, but I must say this one is literally amusing," says Brandon.

Kim tells the man on top of her that she feels really uncomfortable and he gets off of her and helps her up at the same time.

"Thanks" says Kimberley.

The man keeps staring at Kimberley as she brushes off and fixes herself. Alexander and Brandon is looking at him with an intense stare because the man did not let go of Kim's hand.

"Have we meant before?" asks the man.

Kim looks up at the man and replies, "No."

Kim tries to remove her hand from his hand, but he asks her again this time adding on that she reminds him of the daughter of a man who use to work in Australia as a computer genius.

Kim looks down at the floor and tries to pull her hand away because she knows if the man knew about her father there is 100% chance he is working for the enemy.

Still trying to release her hand she hisses when his grip gets tight and tears starts to form in her eyes. A deep smack is heard and the man is laying on the floor grunting. Arms wraps itself around Kim and she sinks into the warm embrace.

"Go into my Office and close the door, I will be right there," says Alex in a soothing voice.

Kim bolts to Alex Office as soon as he lets her go. Outside she hears yelling and other noises.

"I am coming back for you, you hear me, I am coming back for you," Kim hears the man yells as, what sounds like him being drag out by Security.

Kim drops to the floor in fear and starts sobbing, after all that work of making sure she stays off the grid, she is still running into people who are associated with the people who murdered her father. Arms was wrap around Kim and lifts her from the floor to the couch.

"Talk to me Kim, tell me what's going on," says Alexander.

"I can't Alex, as much as I want to, I am not ready to talk about my past," Kim tells him.

Alex nods his head and speaks again saying, "Whenever you are ready, I will be here."

As the day goes by, Kimberley gets settle into her new environment. Working hard, by the time she is finish, lunchtime comes around. Checking the time, she notices it is 2:30 pm and heads out for lunch across the street. Sitting down at the table she starts to sketch the people around her.

"May I take a seat Kimberley?" asks a soft voice.

Kim looks up from her sketch pad to see Kerry Diaz and with a smile she replies, "O course."

"So how is work going" Kerry asks.

"It started off crazy but when the work load came it was great. It took my mind off of things and I am happy," Kim replies to her in a happy tone.

Kerry smiles at Kim's answer and they continue to talk until lunch is over.

"Well I have to go back to the Office, it was nice talking to you Mrs. Diaz," says Kim as she stands up from her seat.

"Please call me Kerry, there is no need for formalities dear."

Kim laughs and hugs Kerry, then she says, "It is nice having someone to talk to."

Kim makes her way to the Conference room and sets it up for Alexander's meeting. After putting together the equipment for the presentation, she sits down and her mind wonders off to this morning and the man who she killed. Kim is so deep in her thoughts that it takes her a while to hear that her phone is ringing.

"Hello, I am calling for Ms. Jones," says the person on the phone.

"This is she, may I ask who is calling?" Kim questions in a curious tone.

"Ms. Jones I am Neil Cooper, Am calling to talk to you about your father."

Kim gasps and replies in a low angry tone, "If you are calling to mess with me..."

The man cuts her off by saying, "Look I know you do not trust everyone who says they know your father, but trust me when I say you are going to want to hear what I have to say, please this is important Ms. Jones." There is a long pause until Kim agrees to see him next week.

In the meeting Kim could not help but think about Neil Cooper and his relationship with her father. She asks herself, "Where they friends or Business partners? Should she trust her instinct?"

After the meeting is over, Alexander comes up to her and asks her about the presentation, but she is still in deep thought as she mutters Neil's name under her breath. Without a notice or warning, Kim feels lips against her own and notices she is being kiss by Alex. After a few moments she gives in and kisses him back which becomes intense.

When they pull apart, they are both panting and Kim speaks, "You just steal my first kiss."

Alex smirks then whispers into her ears, "I know and only I can do that to you, you want to know why?"

Still panting Kim nods and Alex replies, "Because you are mine Kim, your heart, your mind, your body, your everything thing is mine and I do not like to share with no one.

Alex walks to the door then he turns around, "Oh and Kim, Welcome to Diaz Incorporation."

CHAPTER 9

It has been a week working in the Diaz Incorporation and to say Kimberley is exhausted is an understatement. Not only has Alexander have her on her feet, but he also keeps a close eye on her, making sure nobody tries to mess with what is his.

Kimberley could not believe that Alexander stole her first kiss just to make a point. Now he is making sure nobody is in a 5ft radius of her, which is basically why she have her own office because as he states, "The department have all men.

Getting up, she gets David ready for school but a message pop up on her phone indicating she have an Email causes her to stop what she is doing. Thinking it is Alex telling her to come to work she opens it only to see it is from the school.

"Due to the pipes bursting, School is close until further notice."

B   e   s   t

R   e   -

gards,

Principal

"Well, this puts a change in my plans," she says as she looks up at her brother.

"KJ, What are we going to do now? There is no more field trip now that School is close," says David in disappointment.

"No way buddy, since you can not go on your field trip with your friends, How about just the two of us go on our own field trip? You can choose the place."

Putting his pointing finger under his chin, David rubs as his finger back and forward as he thinks. "The Beach sounds like a good idea, we haven't been to one in a long time," he says with a smile.

Kim smile is as bright as the sun as she tells David, "Munchkin, that is the best idea ever."

Kimberley and David arrives at the beach where David dash out to the sand to start building sand castles. Kim sets down her beach bag and lays out two towels, then she opens her umbrella for shade.

"David do you want something to eat or drink?" she asks causing him to stop what he is doing.

He turns around and shouts, "Not now."

As David continues to play, Kim takes out the equipment she needs for painting. Ever since she was young, she would paint different places or paint portraits of her family before her mom past. Her Dad would take the paintings but she never knew what he did with them, when she would ask he would say, "They are in a safe place."

Even before she got the Job at Diaz Incorporation, she would make some cash for her paintings. Smiling to herself, she takes in the view of her brother playing in the water and starts to paint. After an hour, she is finish with a her work and wraps up the painting then joins David.

"David come look at this," says Kimberley as she beckons him over, and when David comes near her she splash's water on him.

David squeals and splash's water back onto Kim which causes them to have a water fight. They are running around playing, when a group of boys shows up disturbing their fun.

"Hey babe, wanna join us?" One of them asks.

When Kim is about to answer, David grabs her hand and pulls her away while he answers the boys saying, "No thank you!"

One of the boys comes up to Kim and says, "Awe, don't be like that honey, send the little one to a Nanny and come party with us."

David yells "She is not your honey, now can you please leave my sister alone?"

"Little boy the grown ups are talking so stay out of it," then he pushes David who falls on the ground.

"Hey!" Kim shouts and pushes the boy who push David, then picks up David who has a bruise on his elbow.

"How dare you push my little brother?" Kim asks with venom in her voice.

"Well, if the little pest would mind his own business he would have been alright," says one of the boys say as he shrugs.

Kim is shock to her those words come out of the boys mouth, "What kind of people hurts a little boy and blames him? she asks herself. With David in her arms, she walks away but the boy who push David is so persistent that he follows Kim and pulls her back.

"Let me make it up to you honey by taking you to dinner, then we end the night at my house," says the one who push David.

"You know I would think your family taught you some manners but apparently these days you children do not know the meaning of the word no, and you disgust me. To watch you treat a child like that, leaves me in more disgust," Kim says as she stares at the boy in anger.

"Listen here you little b..." the boy is about to say but Kim cuts him off.

"No you listen to me you sick, no manner prick. You have five seconds to take your little crew and leave or it will be a problem," Kim says as she gets up in his face.

Smirking, the boy asks, "Do you know who I am? I can ruin you for those words."

"No she does not know who you are, but I do and I can make you regret messing with that poor girl Connor," an angry voice says from behind Kim.

When everyone turns to see who it is, they are grace with Charles and Kerry Diaz presence. Kerry who is standing there with a smile tells Kim to grab her things and join them in their private section.

Kim rests David down and they both gather their things and follows them. The boys just stare at them, because they know the Diaz too well to know they were not the people to talk back to.

Kerry and Kim talk until they reach the private area, where Alexander is standing with his back towards them. His swim trunks are dangerously low and Kim stares at him, looking at how muscular he is.

Alexander can feel eyes on him, so he turns around and sees Kimberley who is in her yellow bikini showing off her curves. A squeal comes from Melissa who is at the bar, then she runs over and hugs Kim causing her to laugh.

"What are you doing here?" Melissa asks and before Kim can reply Charles cuts in.

"Bradley Andrews second son Connor and a few of his friends were harassing her and David, so since we are well acquainted with her, we decide to have her join us."

"Where are they? I need to teach those boys a lesson," Alex says as he clenches his teeth.

In a sweet tone Kerry says, "Calm down Alex, they are al-right," then she bends down to David's level and says, "Come on lets get that elbow clean up, so that it wouldn't get infected." Grabbing his hand they go to where the first aid kit is.

Alex leads Kim's hand to the bar and helps her up on the stool, "Do you want something to drink?" Alex asks.

Kim replies, "A root beer soda would be nice."

Kim's order causes Alex to raise an eyebrow, seeing his reaction causes Kim to tell him, "I do not drink alcohol."

Charles who is watching Alex and Kim from a distance, smiles at how Alex mouth twitches trying to hold in a smile. It is the first time in years Alex is smiling and his eyes that was stone cold have life in them. Charles could not help but feel like a protective father over Kim, he watch her and it feels like something has her cautious, like something or someone is trying to hurt her but she is hiding it from everyone that is around her.

"Uncle Charles, it looks like you are seeing wedding bells the way your eyes is glowing," Melissa says.

"Tell me about it, Dad never look this excited with Alex and his relationships until now," Evan the oldest son says.

The family gathers in the private area where they meet and talk to Kim. They spend the whole day together until it is time to pack up and leave. Kim picks up David who falls to sleep a while ago and makes her way to the car.

"Let me walk you to your car Kim," Alex says and they starts to walk to the parking area.

"Your family is very interesting," Kim says with a smile.

Alex laughs and says, "I going to have to agree on that, imagine growing up with them."

Kim laughs and Alex turns to stand in front of her. Rubbing the back of his neck, Alex looks into her eyes then asks, "Would you like to go on a date with me?"

Kim is in shock as she stare at him with a mouth ajar, after a few seconds she smiles and says, "I would love to."

Breathing a sigh of relief he asks, "How is Saturday?"

Kim replies, "Saturday is fine."

As Kim gets David ready for bed, she tucks him in and kisses him goodnight. Then she makes her way to her bedroom. Getting ready for bed she stands in the shower with a smile thinking about today and what is to come Saturday. When she comes out of the bathroom, she makes her way to the bed and her cell phone goes off. She answers it and on the other side it is Neil.

He says, "I can not meet you Friday Kimberley because I am taking care of some business but a month from now we can meet up, be careful Kim it is a very cruel world we are living in," with that he hangs up.

Kim stares at the phone then she lays down, having terrifying thought which consumes her mind, with that she falls to sleep.

CHAPTER 10

Sitting at her desk, Kimberley goes through the system to see if the firewall and other amenities are in place. Walking into the elevator, Kimberley makes her way up to Alexander office to give her report of how the system is running smoothly.

The elevator opens and in walks a woman that could be straight from vogue magazine wearing Gucci from head to toe. She has on so much Gucci, you would think she is the poster woman for their brand.

When the elevator stops on Alexander's floor, Kimberley walks out and heads straight for his office. What in, she holds up the file and says, "I have the report for you on the progress of the..." but before she can finish a high pitch voice interrupts her.

"Aly baby, I thought you don't allow people to walk in your office without knocking or is she more than your worker, possibly a bed warmer, says the screeching voice of the woman in all Gucci.

"What the hell did you just call me?" Kim asks in disbelief.

"Hillary what are you doing here?" I thought I told you I never want to see your face again," says Alex interrupting Kim who is about to tell this woman off.

"But baby we are still together and I need you to come to my parents house, they are dying to meet you, is Saturday okay for you?" Hillary says in a sultry tone and tries to look seductive.

Alex clenches his teeth before he replies, "No."

Hilary yells, "No! What do you mean no?"

Alex puts up his pointing finger and says, "Number one, we were, are and will never be together, you made that choice when you slept with my number one enemy and number two, I have a date with my girlfriend."

"Girlfriend?" Hillary screams causing both Alex and Kim to flinch. Slamming her hand on the desk she asks, "Who is she? She can't be better than me."

Kimberley who is standing there watching is beckon by Alex to come towards him where she is pull into his lap, then he kisses her neck and looks at Hillary with an eyebrow raise.

"Unbelievable," Hillary says as she throws her hands in the air, she goes on to say, "I just got stood up for a nobody, or should I say a whore.

"Excuse me Ms. Devil in Gucci who is apparently the face of the brand, prostitute that gives it up for free of charge, I have never been with a man in my life so slandering my name calling me a whore, you either need to check the mirror or is your face that scary that the mirrors put themselves back in the store, Kim says clapping back to Hillary.

Hillary has her mouth drop open and as she is about to say something to Kim, Alex kicks her out and threatens her with having Security do the job for her. She left after giving Kim a glare that if looks can kill, she would be dead.

About 4 seconds after Hillary left Alexander burst out laughing, "I can't believe you just told her that," he says amuse.

"Well she looks like she needs to be knock off her high horse," Kim says as she shrugs.

Kim pauses for a moment going into deep thought then asks "Did you really have to tell her I am your Girlfriend?"

"Yes, because she needs to know unlike her I am comitted to you," he says as he kisses her cheek.

"Alex we haven't even went on our first date yet," Kim says groaning as she puts her head into his chest.

"Then be my Girlfriend and our first date will be the start of our relationship," says Alex who lifts up Kim's head as he rubs her chin.

"You do realize we have not known each other for that long?" Kim asks tilting her head to the side looking at Alex.

"That does not excuse what I feel for you and it is not infatuation, it is more than that, I can't explain it but it is there," says Alex who is looking at Kim with what she assume is love.

Kim gets up and walks around the table. Heading to the door she stops then turns around, "I will be your Girlfriend after I see how our date goes on Saturday, and with that she walks out.

Alexander leans back into his seat then looks up at the ceiling with a big smile, he plans to make this date memorable and win over Kim's heart. Where as Kimberley, works all day thinking about everything that has happen and hopes that she can have somewhat of a fairytail ending.

The days went by fast and before Kimberley can say what's that, it is already Saturday. Kimberley gets ready in a above the knee, length navy dress with open toe silver shoes and silver jewelry.

She styles her hair by pulling it into a bun and applies her makeup neatly. She makes a note to thank Melissa for teaching her how to do lady like things, because if it wasn't for their online chats, she would have never knew how to apply makeup. The door bell rings and Kimberley makes her way downstairs to open the door.

Standing there dress in soft grey pants and a white button down shirt with the sleeves roll up is Alexander. He has roses in his hand and a smile on his face, "Wow you look beautiful Mi amore."

Kim blushes at his words and beckons him inside, telling him, "You are not too bad yourself Mr. Diaz."

"Where is David? He asks with curiosity.

"He receive an invite to his best friend sleepover that I happily agree to, after a few questions to make sure he is safe while in the care of another," Kim replies.

Alex nods his head then hands her the roses, so that they can be place in a glass of water. "You sound happy that he is at sleepover," Alex points out then he walks closer to her. Standing in front of her, he asks her with a smirk on his face, "Is it because of me?

Kim laughs and answers, "No, it is mostly because David was sick a lot, he never really had a chance to go to school and have friends. I mean he could have because my Dad could have told the school about his medical problem, but my Dad did not want to send him. It was his way of protecting David."

Alex grabs Kim's hand and leads her to his car. Making sure she is in he makes his way to the driver's seat and puts the car in motion. After a ten minute dive, they pull up to a nice Restaurant, in which they enter.

"Table for two under the name Diaz," he tells the Hostess and they were taken to a table beautifully decorated.

They sit down and starts their order off with entrées and soft drinks. While they wait, they play twenty one questions.

"Alright, so what is your favorite color? asks Kim.

Alex smiles then replies, "Royal blue. "What is yours?" he asks.

Kim replies, "Deep purple."

"Favorite sport?" she asks him.

"Boxing," he replies.

"No way, I seriously thought you were a football type of guy," she say in awe.

Alex laughs at her then he asks, "What is your favorite sport? Please do not tell me football."

"Nope, I am more of a soccer type of girl," she answers.

"How old are you?" she asks.

" I am twenty five, I would ask you about your age, but that would be a rhetorical question seeing that I read your resume," he says.

"And you would be correct," she says.

"So in that case, where do you see yourself in the nearest future?" he asks.

The waiter comes with their order and they continue their conversation. "I see myself at a good place where I am at the pinnacle of my success, married to the man I am in love with and we are having our first child. David will be living the life that he wants as he transitions into pre-teen or a teenager. I never see myself with a big mansion because the place I call a home, is one that is build with love, trust, and happiness," Kim says as her eyes fill with water.

Grabbing Kim's hand, he holds it and asks, "Kim will you be my woman? You have everything a man like me wants, no correction, you have everything a man needs, what I need in my life. So I am asking not for you to be my girlfriend because that is for children, will you be my woman," he asks again.

As the tears flow down her cheeks, Kim replies, "Yes, Ii will be your woman, if you be my man.

"Absolutely," he tells her.

As the night goes by, Kim and Alex becomes closer and when he drops her back, she lets him walk her to the door but before she can go inside, she kisses him passionately. When they pull apart, they go their separate ways bidding each other goodnight.

Chapter 11

I t has been a month since Alexander and Kimberley started
dating and to say that it is bliss is an understatement. She
was surprise that he ask her to attend a banquet that was
suppose to be this month, but was postponed three months
from now due to complications with the guest list.

Watching Alexander speak to his clients in the meeting,
she is in deep thought about how lucky she is to have a
smart, handsome and sweet man in her life. After the meeting
is done, Alexander pulls Kimberley into a kiss. Her stomach
have butterflies because in her mind the kiss is slow and
passionate.

"This is something I can get use to," Alex says pulling away
from Kim.

"Oh really Mr. Diaz, then if you want more of this, I suggest
you hurry up with your meeting with the staff from England,
Kim says and peck his lips.

Cleaning up the meeting room Kim's phone starts to ring causing her to answer it.

"Ms. Jones, it is time for us to finally meet," the voice says.

Kim recognize the voice as Mr. Neil Cooper and gladly agree writing down the place. Kim makes her way out of the building and starts her journey to the Mexican Restaurant. When she arrives fifteen minutes later, she is greeted by not only Neil but an Unknown man as well.

"Hello Mr. Cooper, I am Kimberley Jones I am here because you have information about my father."

"Yes please sit Ms. Jones, we have many things to discuss," Mr. Neil says as he pulls out a seat for her.

Kim squints her eyes in confusion, "Oh am sorry I thought this discussion is private, may I ask who is this?" she asks in suspicion as she looks at the unknown man.

The man chuckles and gets up, holding out his hand, "My name is Sirus Beckford, I am a close acquaintance of Mr. Cooper and I met your father before."

Kim looks at them curiously but gets down to business, "So what is this secret you know about my father?"

Neil takes a sip of his drinks, the says, "Tell us what you know about the software he created and we will tell you if you hit the nail on the head."

"When I found out about my father's software it was after his death, but he did mention that if it falls into the wrong hands, privacy as we know it would not be possible," Kim says.

"You're correct, the software you are taking about is called the pyramid eye, it has the ability to hack any computer remove the firewall and collect all information. Also, it can also spy on persons who have devices with camera and the thing is nobody knows that the software is there because it is invisible. Any attempts to remove it will shut down the computer by literally releasing a dangerous computer virus," Neil says as he looks at Kim with a serious face.

"I can see why my father wanted that software to be safe, but why did you two have to talk to me in person, am pretty sure a phone call could have been convenient," Kim says with an eyebrow raise.

Sirus cuts in and says, "We know you are looking for the software so we want to make a deal with you, we will give you information on the people who kill you father, but you have to give us the software once you have locate it."

There is silence until Kim starts laughing, then her face becomes furious. She stands up and says, "So you are trying to get your hands on my father's work just like the fools who..." she stops before she says too much. She gets up to leave them without bidding them a goodbye.

"Ms. Jones wait, please stop, I need to give you this," Sirus says.

Kim turns around and looks at Mr. Beckford hand, "What is this?"

He replies, "This is more news about your father's case in Australia."

Kim takes the falshdrive but before she could pull her hand away, Sirus kisses her on the lips. Kim pushes him away and slaps him hard.

"Goodbye Mr. Beckford, it seems you have no manners at all, I have a boyfriend who I do not plan on being unfaithful to" and with that she leaves

Kim makes her way back to the office where she discovers that Alexander is looking for her.　　"Where did you go? I have been trying to call you," Alex asks in worry.

"I had a personal meeting with someone, but now that am available lets go out," she says as she wraps her arms around him.

"Where to?" He asks embracing her as well.

"Anywhere" she answers and they heads out.

Alex and Kim watch movies together on his love seat, but the only thing on Kim's mind is, "Should she or should she not tell Alex about everything, from her past to what happen today."

Chapter 12

Neil, Sirus, and Kimberley have been having private meetings ever since she looked at the flash drive. They were discussing plans to locate the software and from there they would see what action they would take.

"Excuse me, I know these people are dangerous but two wrongs do not make a right. We are not going to get rid of anybody, the better alternative to do is turn them in to the authorities, are we clear?" Kimberley says as she looks at both Neil and Sirus sternly.

Neil smile and says "Of Course."

"By the way, why do I have a feeling that this Software contains more than you are telling me," says Kimberley with an eyebrow raise.

"Well, this software was tested and…" Neil's starts to say but Sirus cuts him off.

"And I think it is time for you to head out to the important meeting you mention earlier."

Looking at his watch, Neil murmurs then gets up saying, "You would think after rushing you two and telling you that you we only have an hour and a half to brainstorm, I would keep track of time."

After Neil left minutes ago, Sirus and Kimberley starts to clean up. The room is a too quiet for Kim, looking at Sirus she decides to speak braking the silence.

"So tell me something about yourself."

Sirus stops and looks at her, smiling he asks, "Are you trying to make conversation or are you tired of whoever your boyfriend is and trying to get a taste of Sirus?"

Kim laughs and replies, "If I were over my boyfriend, you would not be my other option."

"Ouch that hurts," Sirus says placing his hand on his chest.

The room becomes quiet again until Kim looks over and sees Sirus struggling with an arm full of trash. Putting together her set of garbage, she walks close to Sirus.

"Here let me help you," she goes to reach for his trash and because of his sudden movement the trash that had a cup with half of alcohol in it falls on her blouse staining it.

"Crap my apologies Kim, here let me help you get clean up," Sirus says as he directs Kim to a room.

After a while Kim returns with one of Sirus shirts on her, "Thanks for the shirt, I will return it tomorrow," she says fixing it properly.

Looking out the window, he takes in the view before saying to her, "You know your father was a good friend of my father, but they weren't as close as his other friend."

"Other friend?" Kim asks in confusion, but since Sirus have his back to her, she walks to the side of him and looks out the window. Then she continues saying, "I never saw any of my Dad friends, as a matter of fact, he never kept friends because he thought they would betray him like always."

Sirus turns to Kim who mimics his action and for a second they were staring into each other eyes, until he leans in to kiss her. Kim turns her head and his lips falls on her cheek.

"Look Sirus you are a great man, but I am in love with my boyfriend and I picture a future with him. Maybe one day you will have a nice girl in your life but it can't be me, you know thinking about it I have a friend back in Australia who will love to date you."

Sirus laughs and says, "You are really something Kimberley Jones."

Kim walks to the door and then turns around, "Goodnight Sirus, am glad I get to meet someone other than my boyfriend, his family and friends."

Sirus smiles and says, "Me too, goodnight Kim."

Sirus turns back to the window and thinks to himself, "Is this really what I want to do? I can't trust her, because she can be just like her father."

Walking up to her door she keeps thinking about Sirus, something did not feel right about him. Hearing noises causes her train of thoughts to be broken and when she opens it, she sees the most beautiful scene ever. Alex and David are playing, they set up a Fort and her pots, utensils and what looks like chips are scatter all over.

"KJ your home," David says running to her.

She picks him up and asks, "What is going on?"

"I decided to come over but only the Babysitter and David were home, so I relieved her and had a boys night with this little guy," he says pointing at David.

A smile makes its way on her lips and she tells Alex, "That is the sweetest thing that anybody has ever done. I am so happy that you and David are bonding."

A yawn passes David's lips as he says, "KJ am sleepy."

This causes Alex to take him out of Kim's arms and carry him to bed. Kim smiles to herself, thinking about how lucky she is to have a man like him in her life.

After a while, Alex joins her on the love seat snuggling until he speaks, "Where were you tonight?"

This makes Kim go stiff next to him, then she says, "I have been dealing with some personal issues."

"It has been weeks that I either call you or come by and your not home, is there something you are keeping from me?" he asks looking at her.

Kim thinks about telling Alex the truth about everything, but for his safety she decides to lie hoping he would not see through it.

"I have been busy with my painting, you remember when I said that it would be good to have it in a Gallery. Well I am making sure everything is perfect, I also had to make sure the software is updated amongst other things so I have been busy, but that all change now because I am here with you.

They starts to kiss and Kim could not shake off the guilt for lying to the man she loves. As they pull away, Alex mentions the Company annual party celebrating their success and how he wants her to accompany him as his date.

Kim smiles and says, "Yes" and pulls him in for another kiss. They spend the whole night together in each other arms but Kim could not shake off the feeling that something is about to go horribly wrong.

As Alex is sleeping, Kim's phone goes off indicating a message come through and when she opens the message it reads,

"Keeping secrets are not good because you never know who can expose you. Beware Kimberley ."

-- A close Frenemy

Kim starts to hyperventilate causing Alex to wake up and ask, "What's wrong?"

Kim shakes her head and says, "Nothing, just a bad dream, go back to sleep." She closes her eyes and says in her mind, "I will tell him after the party, but for now relax.

CHAPTER 13

Standing in the elevator waiting for it to stop, Kim could not help but wonder if it is a good idea keeping secrets from Alex. She could not shake off the feeling that something bad is about to happen and she will be the center of it all. As the doors open, yelling can be heard from Alexander's office.

"Again!" Kim thinks, "It seems that this man always like to start his morning like this."

Walking into his Office to see what's the problem, she sees a fuming Alexander. "What's going on?" Kim asks.

Jared who is on the computer tells her, "Somebody hack the system and stole valuable files, it seem that they use a backdoor computer before they got into the company then sent a virus that shut down the entire system."

Kim is mortified that all her hard work of keeping the companies computer network safe is jeopardize by someone. She decides to volunteer to look at the system to see if she can pull the IP address and catch the culprit. After gathering information she makes her way to her office and gets to work immediately.

After hours of working, Kim starts to notice something about the Hackers Internet Address. It matches the same one as on the computer she uses for the company.

"How is this possible?" She asks herself in shock.

Everything leads back to her and she have no idea how she could be the hacker. She notices that money, new plans for the company and a list of upcoming clients were stolen. If this were to be reported to the police, the responsible party would go to prison.

A loud knock is made at the door and she tells the person to, "Come in."

Jared walks in and tells her, "There is an important meeting right now, it is an emergency."

She gets up and makes her way to the meeting room for Staffers where she sees a furious Alexander standing on stage with his father, Brandon and other men.

"Good afternoon, today we discovered that someone hacked our computers and collected important information from us. We figured it is our competitors and just a while ago it was confirmed. Today Beckford Enterprise announce some of our products and have had a meetings with some of our clients. We lost all of our work because of the virus that was uploaded. Now anyone who have been found betraying our company by working with Beckford will be fired and remove from all of our amenities."

As Alexander is speaking, Kim is trying to figure out why Beckford sounds familiar until she hears Alexander say, "Sirus Beckford will pay for his crimes."

She runs to the bathroom and empty the contents of her stomach, she can not believe that Sirus is behind the hacking and now it starts to make sense. They hack it through her company computer and the virus was uploaded through the flash drive.

Kim makes her way out of the building bumping into everybody she passes. She finds Beckford Enterprise and runs inside. With the help of the Receptionist she finds his Office and without knocking, barges in.

"How dare you use me to get information from Diaz Incorporation Sirus Beckford, are you really that selfish? I could go to prison for this," she says with venom.

Sirus looks at her then dismiss the people in the room. "Listen Ms. Jones, our companies have been head to head since our Grandfathers founded it, so it's nothing personal."

"Did I hear you right? Damn you to hell, I have work so hard to be where I am at and for you to take it away after wanting my fathers work, I am starting to think that if I did decide to locate and give you the software, you would use it against me and since you are enemies with Diaz Incorporation it would

be a bonus prize to bring them to their knees, am I right?"
Kim says angrily.

Sirus looks at her for a moment, "Let me escort you out
of the building and after you cool off we can have this
conversation later."

Sirus gets up and leads her out the building to her car in
the park in lot, "Am sorry Kim but this is how the business
world runs, well my business world to be exact, you will never
understand and I am pretty sure that Alexander's company
can make a comeback, it always do."

Kim looks at him as if he is the most stupid man on earth
and says, "Are you serious, do you realize that I can loose
everything I worked for and be label as a traitor because
some idiot decides it will be good to use a vunerable girl to do
his dirty work unknownly and now he is standing here telling
me there is still a comeback for the company. You know what
I have heard enough, good bye Mr. Beckford," she jumps in her
car and speeds away.

Walking into the Office, she sits down and decides she
should come clean and leave because this is far from over.
But the stupid side of her is telling her to attend the company party tomorrow and maybe Alexander will not be upset.
Kim gets another unknown text from the same number that
scared her last night, so she opens it up.

"It's not good to keep secrets when you know it's going to blow up in our face, enjoy the party tomorrow because you never know when it's your last."

--Frenemy

CHAPTER 14

Kim remain busy the whole week trying to reverse the damages made by Sirus and Neil. She went out and got herself a new laptop, then she started making some calls to all of the Diaz Incorporation clients where she held meetings in private so that nobody knows what she is doing. She even found a way to get the money that was stolen, transferred back to the Company.

"Kim can you hear me?" She hears Melissa ask through her trance.

"Yeah, I was thinking about somethings that came up," she replies.

After a short pause she asks Melissa, "Tell me what you know about Sirus Beckford?"

Melissa have a look of confusion on her face, then she asks, "Why?"

Kim bites her bottom lip before she stares at her and says, "It's complicated to explain now, but when I put all the pieces together, then I will tell you."

"Well, all I can say is that he can never be trusted. He will do anything to bring down the Diaz family, after all his hatred was pass down from his Grandfather," Melissa says.

Seeing Kim facial expression, she continues by saying, "Let me start from the beginning, while his Grandfather hated Alexander's Grandfather, their fathers were bestfriends. Sirus Grandfather use to steal from Alex Grandfather so they were enemies. Eventhough they tried to keep them apart when they were growing up, Uncle Charles was a good friend with Sirus father, that is until they meant a boy name Edward Jones who help both their company succeed."

Kim can not believe her ears when she hears her father's name being call. This is probably why she was told by him to move to New York, maybe she was suppose to meet the Diaz father.

"Tell me why did they stop being friends if they were close, because I am pretty sure they both were trying not to follow in their father's footsteps?" Kim asks eagerly.

"One day Edward told Charles he was going to make him something that will help his company blossom, a generous donation for helping him meet a lovely young lady name Mary. When Sirus's dad heard about this, he stole Edwards work, released it under his company and all of the plans

Edward and Uncle Charles created was honored in Sirus's dad name. He did not acknowledge none of them causing them to not only break their friendship up, but also they became sworn enemies," Melissa says in one breathe.

Tears starts to flow down Kim's face because of what she is hearing, her father had been betrayed so many times no wonder he kept his children and work a secret. Eventhough he hired Stephen, he still kept an eye out but low and behold, Stephen was a backstabber too.

Kim looks at Melissa and says, "Melissa I need you to promise me something."

"What do you want me to promise you?" She asks in a confuse tone.

"That whatever happens you will look after David for me, be there for him, I know it sounds crazy but something is going to happen, don't ask what, just know that I am clueless as a fish but I would never betray Alexander nor his family," she says as she looks at Melissa with a serious face.

"Kim, you are freaking me out, if you are in trouble I will stand by you and help. Tell me what is going on because I can see something is stressing you out," Melissa says in a panic.

Grabbing her hands and raising them up, Kim says, "The less you know the better, I should have taking a page from my father's book when he said to learn who to trust and not. Please, just promise me without any questions."

Melissa eyes start to become watery as she tells Kim, "I promise, but if there is any sign that you are in danger, I am gathering my A team and coming for you."

Laughing as she wipe her tears, Kim says, "Agree!"

As she is getting ready, Kim hears a knock at the door and goes to answer it. There Alexander stands in all his Adonis glory causing her heart to skip three beats and in her mind, she is doing somersaults.

"Damn how did I get lucky?" She hears Alex ask.

"I was about to ask the same thing," she say with a smile.

"You look beautiful," he says.

Blushing, she smile and says, "You do not look too bad yourself."

"Shall we?" he extends his elbow out for her.

She grabs on and says, "We shall."

Arriving at the party she is greeted by a happy Kerry and Charles who are excited that she come to the party. Alexander left to talk with the clients that he thought he had lost when the company was hacked.

Looking around she spots Brandon and Melissa dancing and goes over to talk to them when she is stop by a woman old enough to be in set with her mother.

"I have to speak to you in private, please follow me," the woman says in a whisper.

Kim become curious and scared but for this woman to approach her, whatever she needs to say is extremely important. So she followed her to the ladies room, which is empty.

"What is this about?" Kim asks as she leans on the door just in case she needs to escape.

The lady turns around and says, "I know who you are Kim, as a matter of fact I know all about your father and his past. Have you ever wonder why your father kept you and your brother a secret? or why he became very secretive in his work? When people become greedy, they get desperate, which causes people to become stupid.

"I'm confuse, what does that mean?" Kim asks.

"Be careful of Neil Cooper and Sirus Beckford, they both are dangerous and foolish to think that working together would be beneficial to them. But each one is holding a knife waiting until the other gets sloppy so they can plunge it in their back," with that the woman left.

Kim walks out of the bathroom and goes back to the party where Alexander is giving a speech. Alexander closes his speech by saying, "Enjoy yourselves while I entertain my beautiful girlfriend."

Kim smile when she sees Alexander walking towards her but it is replace when Hillary grabs the microphone and asks for everyone's attention.

"Good Evening ladies and gentlemen, now I know you are all wondering why I decided to crash the party, it is because

Alexander and everyone of you are being played by Kimberley Jones," she says looking at Kim with a smirk.

Anger made its way into Alexander causing him to stomp to where Hillary is standing so he can remove her himself.

"Let me stop you right there Aly baby, you see Kim here has been seeing your rival and she was the one that cause you to lose money amongst other things. If you do not believe me take a look at this."

Pointing at the screen, she shows everyone how Kimberley was meeting Sirus and the time he kissed her. It also shows her walking out of his home with his shirt on. Everything looks as if Kim was a betrayer and unfaithful to Alex and his family.

Alexander turn around to face Kim, "Is this true, please tell me Hillary is making up bull."

Tears starts to flow down Kim's face and when she is about to answer, Jared step in to confirm that what Hillary speak is indeed true. He went on to tell him about the IP address being a match and all his findings pointing to Kim.

With a disgust face Alex march to Kim and yells, "I trusted you and this is how you repay me, how could you do this to me and to my family? I know I should not have never hired you let alone date you."

"Alex please, this is not what it looks like," Kim sobs.

Alex cuts her off by saying, "You are hereby fired from this company, do not come to look for Job letter because I would not put in a good word for you, leave the company car, laptop and phone in the condo when you pack your things and move out. We are done, I never want to hear from you again."

Kim heart break hearing Alex words, looking around she notices everyone looking at her with disgust, including Kerry, the woman that she thought of as a mother figure.

"I am so sorry," she says to everyone then walk out with her head hang low.

Alex stand in the middle of the crowd and tells everyone to go home and he make his way to his Office where she pulls out a bottle of whiskey and starts to drink.

Charles walks into Alex Office and says, "Son put the bottle down, there has to be more to the story and how did Hillary know what Kim had been up to. Something about this does not feel right and although I feel angry at Kimberley, I still have this ache in my stomach that she needs protection."

Looking at his father he says, "Of course Hillary knew what Kim was up to, game recognizes game. Kim is just like her, the only things is she got everyone to love and care for her."

Kimberley is at home packing when Melissa shows up at 10 p.m. at her door. She did not wait for Kim to tell her come in, she just walk pass her and made herself at home on the couch.

"Kim I need you to explain to me why? Because that does not sound like you nor did it look like something you would do."

"I did not betray Alex, Sirus set me up by using me. The pictures that you saw tonight were the meetings we had to discuss why my father was killed. He knew more information about the work my father had and..." Kim says but is cut off by Melissa.

"Let me stop you right there," Melissa hold up her hand and continues, "How do Sirus know your father?"

Kim huff and replies, "Because my father is Edward Jones and now that I know the truth about what he did to him and Charles all those ago also adding on to what he have done to me, I am going to confront that bastard."

Melissa gasps, "Okay Kim since I am the only one who knows what happen to Mr. Jones and now that I know he is Uncle Charles best friend let me help. I would not be surprise if he is in deep with the people who killed your father."

Kim shook her head no, "Let me go alone and if I am not back in an hour then get help. Also, I need you to look after David, he will be safe with someone I trust. Whatever you do, do not come looking for me. I need to put an end to this crap."

"Please be careful Kim," Melissa says in worry hugging her.

Breaking all the traffic laws, Kim arrives at Sirus place and knocks as hard as she can.

"Sirus open the damn door I know you are in there."

Sirus opens the door immediately and says, "Kim what are you doing here? Now is not a good time."

"It isn't? Too flipping bad, you screw me over and now you are going to pay," Kim screams at him.

"Si baby come back to bed," a voice says.

Kim recognize that voice and push past Sirus where she meets a half naked Hillary.

"Well sweet baby Jesus, I knew it, this was all a set up, I should have known that you were never had no interest in helping me with my father's situation," Kim snorts.

Kim crosses her arms and says, "You know Hillary, if you wanted Alexander, you did not have to lay in bed with Sirus to get information to sabotage me. You made me look like a no good whore not to mention a traitor, I hope you are proud of yourself."

"What are you talking about Kim?" Sirus asks.

Kim points at Hillary, "This prada whore of a she devil crash Alexander party and show everybody pictures of us and told everyone I was working as a company spy for you."

"That's impossible Kimberley, Hillary did not know that we were meeting, she did not even know about us contacting each other," Sirus says to her blatantly.

"You are right because I put that plan into action," a voice says behind them.

As everyone looks at the door, they all pale to see who it is and the voice continues by saying, "Now that I finally have what I wanted, I do not need you."

Gun shots went off with the three of them screaming.

CHAPTER 15

"Finding out about Kimberley's betrayal was enough for me to hit the bar and drink because she is just like Hillary, a money hungry slut. Taking some time off I stayed in my father's guess house sulking until my father threw me out and said to get over it."

"Melissa have been trying to call me non stop, but I press the ignore button and head out to work. I make my way into the Office where I find Terry my Assistant waiting for me.

"Sir you have six meetings book today," she says causing me to stop and turn to look at her."

"Meetings? I never schedule no meetings because we lost all of the upcoming clients, I reply looking at her curiously."

"That's it sir, they were schedule to meet last week," she says as she leads me to my first meeting where the clients are waiting. It take about two hours to deal with them and in the end we gain their cooperation."

"Alexander!" I hear my name being call and turn around to see Mr. Wildgoose. Shaking his hand I ask him, how have you been?"

"Good," he nods as he replies, then went on to say, "I am impress with your assistant, when she called and told us what Sirus Beckford did causing your company to lose profits, we met and set this hold thing up. She even upgraded our computer systems and place new protection software on them."

"Yeah! Tara is something I say as I laugh."

"Tara? Who is Tara? The women we talk to name is Kimberley Jones, she help us and in return we come back to you," Mr. Wildgoose says."

"It was Kimberley? I could not believe my ears. I look at him with my mouth open, then excuse myself to see Brandon and Jarod."

"Knowing them, they would be in my Office because we were suppose to have our own meeting to clean up what was destroyed by Sirus. I need you two to, but before I finish they beat me to it."

"All the money that was stolen is back into our account, a women by the name of Kimberley Jones went to the bank teller and asked to speak with her boss. Their they got all the money Sirus stole from you, but since in this situation it took six to nine business days to process we just get notification," Jarod says."

"My dad gets up from the corner and says, "Son it looks like Kimberley tried to fix the problem when she discovered she had been played."

"Damn it, I need to talk to her I say running my hand through my hair."

"Brandon shakes his head, "We have a problem," he says with a serious face and continues, "Kimberley is missing, she left David with Melissa and told her if anything happen to her call the police. She went to confront Sirus but never came back to retrieve her things, this morning we discovered Sirus has been shot in the chest and Hillary is dead. Police found a video of someone dragging Kimberley out and she appears to be injured."

"Looking at my Dad he already knows what I am thinking, he gets up and tells us the car is ready to take us to the hospital. Sitting there, I replay everything that has happen and I wish I had stayed with Kim to let her explain, because of that she is not safe in my arms where she belongs."

"We arrive at the hospital where my mother is waiting for us along with Melissa, David, and my whole damn family! My mother gets up and come towards us as she says, "He is awake and talking to Mike and Frank."

"I huff a breath of relief knowing that my dad contact them. When they walk out of the room, they say they will meet us at the mansion and I know what this mean. Whenever Mike and

Frank do not want to speak in public, it means this situation is deep."

"When we are settle in at the mansion, Mike gets up and kneels down to David picking him up. "Hey buddy I want to show you something," he says as Frank comes with the painting of a portrait that hangs in this house from when I was young."

"Do you recognize this picture?" Mike asks David."

"Yes I do!" David says and then points to each person in the picture as he identifies each. That is Daddy, Mommy, KJ and me when I was a baby."

"My father and I heads snap to David then at each other while my mother gasp."

"My father makes his way to David and takes him from Mike, then he asks David, "Where is your Mother and Father?"

"David eyes well up with tears as he tells us they went to heaven, he goes on to say to us his mother became sick so God took her away to ease the pain and daddy was hurt by bad men who wants to take Kim and do bad things with her."

"So I am correct about who your parents are, but I had to confirm before I tell you all this. Please take David to a private room and do not let him out of your sight," Frank says.

After David left the room, we brace ourselves for what we are about to hear."

"Getting comfortable Frank begins to speak, saying, "When David and Kimberley was very young, their Mother had became sick and months after, she passed away. The autopsy that they had done cause them to discover that she was poison causing Edward Jones to keep Kimberley and David private from his job. This is why David is sick because the poison was given to him when she feed him from her plate."

"And Kim? I ask, I needed to know if someone had attempted to hurt my baby when she was just a baby."

"There are reports of kidnapping with Kimberley but they were caught and said to be working with Neil Cooper. Sad thing is because Neil was not in Australia at the time, no evidence was found," Mike says."

"Neil Cooper? Oh no it can't be," Melissa says causing everybody to turn their heads to look at her. Then she inputs her thoughts saying, "A man by the name of Neil Cooper contacted Kim about her father's work and she had a meeting with him. It was at the same time as when she had the meeting with Sirus."

"What? Why the hell you didn't tell me about this, I say to her in anger."

"Melissa returns my glare and say, "Trust is earn when you can believe that the person they tell their secrets to won't spill it to another. And if I had known the danger she was in, I would have put my foot down and speak out."

"We know about the meetings, Sirus told us about the negotiation he had with Neil Cooper and how after Kim located the software they would hand her over to Valentino and split the profits 50/50," says Mike."

"Who the hell is Valentino? I ask through clench teeth."

"A mob boss who is interested in making Kimberley his bride. He is also the one who they suspect of killing Edward Jones," says Frank."

"My mother gasp before asking, "Do you think she knows that her father was killed by Neil Cooper? Better yet does she knows how her father died."

"Sissy saw when the bad men hurt daddy, she placed me in the closet and I watched cartoons while she looked through the peek hole that she made to watch me when she did her homework and could not stop." We all turn to look at David who is drinking apple juice, my dad bend down and open his arms to pick David up."

"Mike stood in front of my Dad and David and ask, "Can you tell me about the bad man who found you and Kim before you move out of the Apartment?""

" David nods then says, "After we got here a few months later a bad man found us and was chocking Kim but I stabbed him and when he went to come after me, KJ killed him with a big knife then past out."

"When did this happened? I ask shouting."

"Melissa turns her head and answers, "The night before she save Aunty from getting mugged.""

"My mother drop on the couch in tears, Kim had went through a lot," I say to myself. "David I am curious where did you and Kim stay when you first came here? I looked at him hoping he would say the Apartment but boy was I wrong.

"We stayed at a shelter until we moved because a man tried to touch her wrong. We stayed on the streets for two days until KJ found an Apartment then you came along and gave her a job. I have never seen my sister happy until you came, but she was scared to tell you the truth about us because that means you would be in danger too."

"I ball my fist at this because if I had known I would have locked her in my Condo and have someone follow her until I was sure nobody will get to her," I say to myself. I hear my father telling David to let the maid put him to bed where he would come and check on him later."

"Melissa drop on the couch next to Brandon and say, "I should have known, I knew about everything except the shelter and streets but Kim is so stubborn she will suffer before she ask for help or money."

"Pacing up and down Dad stop in the front of me and say, "Son we need to find Kim, Neil is dangerous and he does not play nice, especially since he holds a grudge against Edward."

"How? What do you mean?" I ask."

"My dad looks at me with a disgust face then starts his story. Before any of you were born, Edward, Neil and I was best friends, that is until the Jones family discovered that

Neil was not apart of their family. Their father was drugged by a woman who became pregnant with Neil and as soon as he was born he was left on their doorstep, but after a while Edward mother became pregnant with him."

"When Neil got sick a blood test was run to see if he had any abnormalities, that is when they discovered Neil was not his father's child. Edward immediately became top priority and successor, while Neil was disown and had to take his mother's last name. That is when he became hostile towards Edward, even when Kim's mother chose Edward over him that was the drawing line."

"I remembered he was fascinated with her, now thinking back, he was so obsess he tried to abduct her and take her to another country. Your father, Mike, Frank and Edward stop him," my mother says as she places her hand on my father's shoulder."

"I look at Mike who jumps up with a bright look on his face that says he just discover something. "This is what he meant in the letter."

"Who? I ask."

"Frank answers, "Five years ago he send us a letter where he had us promise to keep his family safe if something where to happen. We never knew what he meant nor that he had children but now that we know...."

"My father gets up and finish the sentence by saying, "We are not settling down, we are going to find Kim and keep our promise to Edward."

"I turn away walking to go check on David, I am coming to find you Kim and the person who dear to touch you will pay."

CHAPTER 16

Opening her eyes, Kim finds herself in a strange room with no doors nor windows. Sitting up, she gets up to run to the door only to fall on the floor due to her leg being chain with a heavy duty lock.

Kim starts to cry because she has no clue what happen other than Hillary and Sirus was murdered by Neil. Hearing the lock she sits up and looks at a tall man with tattoos all over his body.

Looking at her the man smile as he says, "Very pretty!"

Kim cries as she moves back against the bed for protection only to see another man walk in and stands next to the man with the tattoos. Looking at Kim then at the man he asks, "What happen to her?"

"She started freaking out when I said she was very pretty, I think she is scared," the man replies.

Looking behind them, she sees the man who she loathes come into the room. "Neil," she says with venom but is slap in reply when he walks up to her.

"You will not disrespect me, now come to the dinner table and look presentable," he spits out.

Kim bites her lip and nods to him and as soon as they left, she runs to the bathroom to clean up as fast as she can, then makes her way to the Dinning room. Approaching the Dinning area she hears yelling and the scream of a woman, fear starts to settle in her stomach until a man comes up behind her and pushes her in.

Stumbling she falls forward in the Dinning room. "Come please have a seat next to me," says the man who is cleaning blood off his knuckles. Kim slowly walks around the table and eases down in her seat.

"So beautiful, I see what Neil is saying, you can bring in so much money, tell me has anyone taken your innocence yet?" The man asks without a care in the world.

Chocking on the water she is drinking, Kim asks to be excuse but feels a hand on her thigh.

"Since your reaction confirm your virtue, I can sell you in the bidding for tonight. Tiffany, get her ready in the most seductive lingerie, she goes up for sale tonight," he says in anger.

As Tiffany is getting her ready, she turns to look in the mirror and can feel bile raise up in her throat. "I look like a whore," she says crying.

Tiffany laughs and tells her, "Get over herself, you either get tough or face the consequences. Listen here, I never once ask for this life but if I didn't become what they wanted me to become, I would have been dead with my child."

Kim gets up and asks with sadness in her voice, "How old is your baby?"

Tiffany turns around with a shock expression and answers, "She is three, no one has never ask me that when they came here, that is probably because they never care about how the other girls are feeling. You are the first, do not let them take away your compassion for others. Do you have any other siblings."

"I have a little brother, he is nine and loves baseball, watching cartoons and hanging out with me," Kim answers.

Tiffany smiles but it does not reach her eyes. Sitting down she asks her, "What is his name?"

Kim smiles and replies, "David," then she asks her, "What is your daughter's name?

Tiffany smile brightens as she replies, "Ariel! Hearing under the sea while I watch Disney channel helped me deliver her properly."

"What do you desire most?" Kim looks at her with a serious face.

Tiffany mouth drops open but she closes it and answers, "To leave this place with my baby girl and never look back. To make sure my daughter know that the world is beautiful and not everyone is bad."

"Awe that is so sweet," a voice says at the door. Turning around they face a women who looks like she can give playboy girls a run for their money.

"Who are you?" Kim is curious to know why this girl did not look like she was captured.

"The name's Reagan and I could not help but over hear you two talking. My dream is to see sunlight again but that can never happen because the doors go with a code that changes every half an hour, so you are stuck here, get use to it," then she walks out rolling her eyes.

"Why can she not see the sunlight? They do let you out right?" Kim turns to Tiffany asking.

She shakes her head no then replies, "Everything is done before sunrise so that people would not get suspicious."

Kim eyes widen then went back to looking sad because she thought there would be a way to get out. Looking up at Tiffany she realizes another presence is in the room.

Kim stands there scared as the photographer takes pictures of her in just the red lace lingerie she has on. Neil gets piss because she is not posing, so he approaches her and goes to grab her but she kicks him in his private area and makes a run for it.

First making her way upstairs where a door is open, she glance around and notices she is not nowhere near America nor Australia and runs back inside where she goes into a Closet and hide amongst the supplies.

"KIM GET THE HELL OUT HERE NOW!" Neil shouts as the footsteps comes to a stop in front of the closet making her hold her breath. Two seconds later Neil breaks down the door and drags her out.

Slap, "How dare you?" Slap, "Do that," Slap, "To me." Neil spits with venom as he continues to slap her.

Kim is crying as Neil drags her out of the Closet and into the previous room. Laying her on a mattress he cuffs her hands and feet to the post. "SMILE NOW," he screams into her face.

"GO TO THE BOTTOMLESS PIT OF HELL YOU DISGUSTING BASTARD," Kim shouts in anger.

"I have an idea," he says in a terrifying voice as he retrieves a knife and walks closer to her. He tears off the rest of the fabric and leaves her bare, making the Photographer snap many pictures.

"I am going to load them up and see what the buyers think," the Photographer says looking at his camera.

Neil gets on top of her and says, "That is your first punishment, your second is to sleep in the basement just like this. He drags her by the hair and throws her down a flight of stairs, thanks to something that was on the floor it save her from a nasty fall, but she realize it is a dead body.

She screams as she realize this is the room where they keep the people they kill. "Where is this place? Where am I Neil?" she asks in fright.

"Oh sweety, your in hell paying for the sins of your father." With that, he closes the door leaving her in an abyss of darkness, naked and cold.

Chapter 17

Sitting in the living room, the Diaz family are waiting for Mike and Frank to grace them with their presence on the new found information. A few seconds later a knock is heard at the door and Alexander who is pacing the floor makes his way there to open it.

Opening the door Alexander is greeted with the serious face of Mike, Frank, an unknown man and the person who he wants to kill for causing Kim to end up in this position, Sirus.

"What the hell is he doing here?" Alex asks through clench teeth and a ball fist that is itching to punch Sirus.

"Look Alexander I know you are piss at me for what I did to Kim but I want to make it right, please do not shut me out, nobody knows Neil better than I do and his hate for Kim's father. I know about his illegally activities and the person who he surrounds himself with, you need me as much as I need you," Sirus pleads.

Alex takes a deep breath and turns around walking away indicating that they should follow him. When they abide, they make their way to the living room where the Diaz family is waiting.

Charles stands up and approach Mike shaking his hand, "I'm glad you can join us, what do you have?"

"We have a big problem, it's worst than we thought," Mike responds with a serious tone.

When Charles looks behind Mike he is furious to see Sirus and is about to kick him out when his son interrupts, telling him that Sirus wants to help since it is his fault Kim is in this predicament.

"I know you hate me right now but please hear me out," Sirus pleads to the family, he pauses for a second to regroup and think on what he is about to say then proceeds to speak. "When Neil approached me about the software that Edward Jones created, he did not tell me his real intentions. What we were suppose to do was help Kim find the software then take it from her and cause her to lose her job so she would not have any income to use against us. We were also suppose to put a man name Mr. Valentino, a mob boss in Australia on her trail," he wants Kim to become his wife.

Getting angry more and more, Alex gets up out of his seat, walks to the wall and punches it so hard that it made a hole. He turns to Sirus with a piss off look, "Continue," he says with venom to Sirus.

For the first time in his life Sirus feels fear because if looks could kill, he would be six feet under from Alexander's expression. "As I was saying I decided to do a background check on Neil, that is when I found out about his connections to dangerous people in Paris. He smuggles drugs, weapons, ammunitions and worst of all humans, especially women and children. It is a possibility he is going to sell Kim or use her as an escort to make money."

What Sirus say is enough to make Alex dash towards him and punch him causing him to drop to the floor. Alex did not give a damn that Sirus is still wounded, all he know is that Kim is in the hands of a man who is going to use her and get rid of her like trash.

Charles comes up behind his son to pull him off Sirus who is bloodied in the face. "Listen Sirus, I only pull my son from you because you are the only one who knows about Neil, but if anything happens to Kim, I will personally make your life a living hell and let my son finish you."

Wiping the blood from his mouth, Sirus nods at Charles words and says, "I Understand."

"I think I have something and you all are not going to like it," the man that is with Mike and Frank says. Everybody turns to him with a who the hell are you face, that's when Frank introduce him as cybercrime specialist Toby.

"I decided to look on the dark web with the help of a few friends and judging by the picture I think I found Kimberley."

He hook up the laptop to a projector so that everyone can see it.

"Oh my God, they have her looking like a prostitute and you can see she is scared by the fear that is in her eyes," Melissa sobs.

Alex is furious at what he is looking at, his baby is dress in lingerie that shows off what no man is suppose to see except for him. He says to himself, "When I get my hands on Neil, I am going to rip him apart for putting her in this position.

Charles is holding his head in his hands muttering, "Edward is flipping over in his grave right now."

Toby shakes his head and says, "That is not the worst picture."

Hearing this, everyone turns to look at him. He clicks the keyboard and nods his head at the screen, "That is the worst picture," causing everybody to look at the screen.

Alex jumps out of his seat and heads into another room quickly, the only thing that can be heard is the sound of furniture breaking and roaring out of his mouth. Kerry gets up and runs to Charles burying her face in his chest saying, "These people are sick Charles, why would they do that to her?"

Charles and Kerry goes into the room that Alex is in only to meet him on the floor pulling the hair on his head. He looks up and seethes, "They have a picture of her naked and cuff to the bed, and to make it worst is that bastard is grabbing her by the hair and is on top of her, when I find him he is dead."

Chapter 18

Hearing the door open, Kimberley looks up to see Tiffany and Reagan standing there with their heads poke in the doorway. "Oh my gosh," Tiffany gasp while Reagan mutters cuss words.

"Come lets get you out of here, can you walk?" Tiffany asks Kim.

Kim nods and with the help of both girls she gets up and makes her way out the room. "Hey lets get you clean up," Tiffany says as she makes her way to the bathroom to retrieve a bucket and rag.

"See I told you there is no escaping, just suck it up, your life is over so do not make it hard for us who are trying to survive. Once one girl acts out we all get punish," Reagan shouts while glaring at her.

Tiffany stands up in front of Kim blocking her from Reagan view and says, "Listen, she is scared and has no clue as to why she is really here, so please Reagan do us a favor and shut the hell up. Am tired of you alway messing with the new girls telling them to suck it up when you tried to kill yourself when you first arrive, you might have suck it up but we will never, so back up and leave Kim alone."

Reagan becomes enrage, you could have hear the tea pot noise from her head going off. "Make sure she is presentable, Mr. Valentino is coming here for her," says Reagan.

"Who is Mr. Valentino?" Kim asks as she looks between Tiffany and Reagan with glossy eyes.

Reagan smirks and replies, "Your new master who bought you, word is he has been looking for you for a year now and can't wait to claim you."

Tiffany jumps out of her seat screaming, "Get out and never come around me nor Kim again."

Reagan laughs and says, "Glad to and I hope to never see Kim's face again."

Looking at Tiffany, Kim says, "I don't get why Reagan is upset with me, what have I ever done to her?"

Tiffany takes a deep breath and turns to Kim, "Because of your actions they gave the girls harsh punishments until it was time to retrieve you. It is not the first time somebody tried to escape so I am use to it. We never had one in a long time. just next time think before you act, am not saying it to be mean but I have seen many girls die because they tried."

Kim lays down and soak it all in because in a few hours her master will arrive causing her life to be over.

"It's time to get up," a harsh voice boom in her sleep causing her to snap her eyes open and look up in Neils face. She whimpers when he pulls her out of the bedroom and into the Dining room.

"Mr. Valentino! Meet your new slave Kimberley Jones," Neil smile as he speaks.

"It is a pleasure seeing you Kim, please have a seat as we discuss your arrangements before we leave the place," Mr. Valentino gets up saying while going to hug Kim. Throughout dinner, Kim keeps glancing at Neil who is looking at Mr. Valentino as if he is trying to figure him out.

"Kim pick a girl who will help you gather your things and get you ready to leave," says Neil who looks to be signing a contract.

"Umm," Kim goes off then picks Tiffany who gets up immediately with her child to help.

As they where packing Kim could not help but adore Tiffany's child, laughing at how sweet she is and praying in her mind that someday, somebody will give her a family.

"Let's get these to Mr. Valentino car," Tiffany says, then looks at her daughter and say, "Come help mommy carry Kim's stuff." Getting outside they reach the car where not only Kim but Tiffany and her little girl as well is push inside.

"Drive," Mr. Valentino says.

"What's happening," Tiffany yells holding onto her child and Kim.

"It is okay mam, we are leaving this place and getting you two to safety, just relax."

The car stops and the door is open by another person. Tiffany gets out with her daughter at her side and Kim comes out after her only to see the person she thought she would never see.

"It can't be," she says before she passes out.

Back at the house, the men runs inside telling Neil and their boss about what transpired with Tiffany, her child and Kim. "What should we do boss" one of the men ask.

Neil only punch the wall in anger and says, "Find them and bring them to me, nobody and I mean nobody screws me over," Neil says.

"Where the hell is the girl I bought?" somebody says in a dangerous tone.

Neil turns around and asks, "Who the hell are you? Because we only had one girl that was sold tonight.

The man growls out, "Yes I know that because I bought Kimberley Jones, my name is Mr. Valentino."

CHAPTER 19

Opening her eyes Kimberley heard people talking around her and felt what felt like a warm hard blanket around her. Looking up her eyes landed on familiar Grey eyes that held hurt, regret, anger but most of all love. Am dreaming aren't I, this can't be real, last time I saw you wanted nothing to do with me, how are you here? Kim whispered. Alexander had his arms wrapped around Kim and when those words came out of her mouth he lean down placing his lips on her softly. Am here baby and am never leaving you, when we get home am making sure to cuff you to me or the bedpost in my room.

Tears came out of Kim's eyes, she could not believe that Alex was here with her, he came for her. Wiping the tears she sits up and fires questions at him, how did he knew where she was? what happen when she was gone? Is David alright? Alex place a finger on her lips and shush her, please relax, David is fine, he is with my mom waiting for you to come home and I will tell you everything after you are taking care of.

Charles who was discussing certain matters with his security team looked over at Alex and Kim noticing that she was awake, he went over to her. Sleeping beauty has finally awaken he said chuckling but after a while his face turn serious, young lady do you know if you father was alive he would have had a heart attack and I would have been dead for breaking a promise to protect you.

Kim bite her bottom lip and scrunch her eyebrows together staring at Charles, he looked at her and smile, let me explain your father was my best friend when we were children and after he met your mother curtesy of my wife playing matchmaker, he got a job offer in Australia that he could not refuse causing him to get marry and start a new life in that country. About eleven years ago he came to me with portraits that he wanted me to have and said to keep them safe, then about a few years ago he came out of nowhere unannounced saying if anything happens to him he has a family that he wants me to look after. I did not know that you and David was what he was talking about but now that I know, I will do everything in my power to keep you two safe.

Looking at Charles Kim smile and spoke, I had figured out you knew my father but with everything that had happened it was had to trust anyone. Then Neil and Sirus came along filling my head with things, then Melissa had told me about the past with my Grandfather along with yours and Sirus, she hang her head down and continued everything seem so messed up until Sirus stabbed me in the back. I thought I could tell Alexander or you but witnessing my father who was killed without mercy, I was afraid because bringing me and my family problems to you could cause danger to come to yours.

A finger went under her chin lifting her head up, Kimberley if you had come to me and my Son we don't care what danger came after, Edward was like a brother, we were family not by blood but by the bond that was created when we were children, that bond would go and will be past down in our family line. Tears welled up in Kim's eyes before it started following hard then sobs came out, Charles embrace her into a fatherly hug, looking at Alex he notice tears was falling from him too but by the way his fist was balled, Charles knew his son will do everything in his power to keep Kim and David under his protection, this meant war for the Diaz family.

Letting her go he place a hand on her face, get some sleep we soon land causing her to nod and lean back into Alex. Her eyelids got heavy with Alex whispering soothing words in her ears she fell asleep soon afterwards. An hour later she felt someone shaking her awake, five more minutes, I haven't got the puppies to the beds, a laugh was heard causing her to snap her eyes open when she realize that it was Alex she blush and covered her face.

Alex smile and spoke, don't hide your face from me your beautiful when you blush, he pulled off the blanket and made her sit up so she can be buckle in for landing. After they landed, they made their way through the airport and to the park in lot where a driver awaits them. When they were seated Kim notice that the security was increased, sensing her discomfort Alex told her it was for protection and they can be trusted.

Pulling up to the Diaz Residence Kerry who was holding David, Melissa and the rest of the family was standing outside waiting for the arrival of their loved ones. Charles was the first to come out, then Alex who turn around and pulled out Kim. As they stood there they could hear cries of joy from Kerry and Melissa as well as David calling Kim's name. When they were close Kerry wrapped her arm around Kim telling her how happy she was that she is back home and safe and how she was take care of her until she was healthy again.

Sitting in one of the guest rooms, Kim was listening to David and the adventures he had with the Diaz family. Kim was happy to hear he was having a good time while she was away, looking up she notice Alex leaning on the wall with his hands in his pockets. Buddy it's time for bed let big sis get some rest then you can be with her all day tomorrow he pick up David and left the room after David said goodnight to her.

When Alex placed David in his bed, he kissed him on the forehead. Alex heard David call his name and looked at him, do you think that they will hurt Kim like they hurt daddy? Alex clench his jaw and said not if I have something to do about it, she will be safe, you will be safe in my care. Then with a sleepy voice David ask, do you like my sister? Alex froze then looked at David, with all my heart , I don't like your sister, I am madly in love with her and with recent events I will protect what's mine.

CHAPTER 20

It has been a week since Kim was rescued and everything is back to normal, except for Alex checking on her every thirty minutes. Kerry and Kim was sitting on the patio in the backyard drinking tea and talking, Kerry was telling Kim about what an incredible woman Kim's mother was. Charles had just arrived and decided to not only check on Kerry and Kim but give Kim information on the men after her.

Hello Mr. Diaz Kim acknowledge his presence, Charles glared at her playfully while pointing a finger, young lady didn't I told you to call me Charles or better yet call me dad, you are family whether you know it or not. Kim smile as her eyes well up with tears and she nodded at his words. Charles handed Kim a folder and ask her if she recognize anybody, opening it she immediately notice the man in a black suit smoking a cigar, this man she pointed at the picture and said if she is not mistaken she help him out when she was thirteen, he was shot in the Alley way and she save him.

As Mike and Frank join to give updates they told Kim that Mr. Valentino may have an obsession with her because of that, they also went on to tell her that judging by the investigation he wants to please his infatuation by making her his wife and will go to great lengths even if that meant illegally getting her. Over my dead body an angry voice lace with venom spoke. Looking around they were grace with Alex presence who stood at the entrance to the backyard.

Dinner will be ready soon Kerry stand and kiss Alex on the cheek as she headed in the house. As everyone followed, Alex walked to where Kim was and scope her up in his arm bridal style then made his way to his room. Laying her on the bed he slowly attach his lips to hers as they kiss slowly yet passionately. He removed his lips from her and went to her ears, you are mine and mine alone, I will not let nobody take you away from me and as I said if I have to trap you in my room I will and kitten you won't be bored he bit on her earlobe causing her to squeal.

Alex she moaned as he trail kisses down her neck speaking sweet words to her, you know this door has a lock if you do not want me to walk in you in the process of my grandchildren being made Kerry spoke as she stand at the door with her arms cross and her lips tugging into a smile. Kim hide in Alex chest as he groan mother and hung his head. Hey Kerry did you tell everyone that dinner is ready Charles said while walking up behind Kerry with David in his arms.

David giggle, daddy look, Kim and Alex sitting in the tree K-I-S-S-I-N-G. Charles put his hand over David face, nothing to see here my boy is finally becoming a man, I was starting to get worried when you did not start dating after Hillary but it's all good. Dad Alex groan while Kim burst out laughing. Let's leave the two love birds alone Kerry said pushing Charles and David out. I have been meaning to ask about Hillary Kim started to say but Alex interrupted her by sealing her lips with a kiss, she is gone so please do not think about her, I feel sorry for what happen to her but she shook hands with the devil.

Biting her lips she nodded but thought to ask him later about Sirus, pulling her up they made their way downstairs hand in hand. Everybody was enjoying themselves until a knock was heard at the door, a goodnight was heard followed by Sirus standing in the dining room doorway. Alex jumped out of his seat, what the hell are you doing here didn't I warn you to stay far away from Kim and when I mean far away, Pluto from Earth.

I get it, but I had to talk to her myself Sirus said putting up his hands. Alex walked up to him, I don't care I am not letting Kim out of my sight and to have you talk to her you will have to knock me out before that happens, so get the hell out. Looking at Alex then at Kim who was being shielded from him by Alex brothers, Sirus hung his head down and said am so sorry Kim and I hope someday you will forgive me for everything, then he turned around and walked out.

Kim stood there not knowing what to do, in her heart it was saying to forgive him and in her mind it was telling her don't trust Sirus because he broke it the moment he played her. Biting her bottom lip she look up to see Alex standing in front of her staring at her. Please don't think about forgiving him Kim and if you do, forgive and never see or be in the same place as him again.

As they went back to eat dinner Alex place his hand on Kim thigh rubbing it up and down, as she suck in a breath she look at Alex who was smirking while he talk about how the company is prospering all she thought was you dirty dog. When dinner was done Kim help out with the dishes then headed to bed where Alex was seated on the bed, what are you doing here? I want to sleep with you, Kim eyes widen say what now she squeak, Alex got up quickly after realizing his mistake, no I mean not as in that way she said scratching his neck.

Kim laugh at him and agreed knowing what he meant making her grab his hand and move to the bed laying them both down. Looking at each other Kim smile at him and said I am glad things are back to normal, somewhat. What do you mean somewhat, Alex ask, I mean there is still people after me and my father's work that I can't seem to find and you always checking on me all day everyday, I just want you to focus on yourself this is my mess.

Kim look at me, this is our problem, when I claim you as mine your problems became mine do you know why? Kim shook her head no then said but Alex kiss her, in that kiss she felt love and passion. That is why, Kimberley Jones I am deeply in love with you, tears came to Kim's eyes and with a smile she said I feel the same, I am deeply in love with you too Alexander Diaz with that they fall asleep in each others arms.

Chapter 21

Alex and Kim walked into the building of Diaz Incorporation early in the morning. Many people were looking at them but mostly telling Kim welcome back because they had heard about what Sirus had done to her and how he drag her into trouble and was the cause of her termination. Sitting behind the desk in Alex office because he was serious about not letting her out of his sight that he made it that they was a desk set up in his personal office for her.

Checking to see if the firewall was in place Kim found a hidden software in one of the files that look like a spyware. Alex take a look at this Kim called him over when Alex rounded the table to see what Kim was showing him she explain the hidden software and ask if he knew about it. Alex got on the phone and called Jared up to his office. A knock was heard followed by Jared walking in and was filled in about the spyware.

Kim left Alex and Jared to work on the problem as she went to the break room for something to snack on. While she ate people started screaming as alarms went off in the building, Kim wondered what was going on because every alarm should not go off at the same time, rushing out she ran into a man who said there is problems in the electric room for the computers making both of them check it out.

When they arrive Kim gasp at how smoke and sparks was flowing in the room, we need to find the breaker for the building and shut the whole thing down for this place goes up in flames. Do you have a laptop she ask the man who nodded and got his immediately, let get to the breaker she said while opening the laptop as they walk. What are you doing the man ask her watching as she walk and work on the laptop, I am hacking into the server quickly before we loose all the data, I know the files backs up to our home computers but that is only after the head approves any recent work will be gone immediately.

As she finish backing up the files Kim got curious about something, Why is everybody else not thinking to shut off the breaker, she quickly did further work then close the laptop. They reach the breaker room and shut down the whole room completely, that was close Kim huff a breath and laugh, yes I know the man said with a sinister smirk then hit Kim in the head with a pipe. Retrieving his laptop, this was too easy who knew I would get the plans the new project Alex was working on he said to him.

Walking out he ran into someone, boss he said more like a question. Did you get it the man questioned, yes I got everything here they played right into my hands he said. The boss walked away causing the man to leave before getting caught. He was smart enough to blend in with the others and walk out with them.

Where is Kim Alex shouted as they exited the building letting the authority do their jobs and since nobody answered he tried to go back inside but was stopped by authorities who told him it wasn't safe. ALEX someone yelled, he turned around looking at his mother and father and went over to them, where is Kim? Kerry ask frantically but got in return a I don't know, she hasn't come out, no one has seen her. Charles called over an officer and told him that a Kimberley Jones is still in the building and to look for her.

Kimberley, Kimberley, wake up your safe now. Groaning Kim open her eyes to see Sirus looking at her with pain in his eyes. Sirus is that you, she ask with her eyebrows scrunch together, what happen she spoke looking around the breaker room. I don't know one minute am entering in the building to look for Alexander to talk to him the next am hearing a noise then seeing a man running out, I came to see what happen and found you here.

My head is hurting, I need to find, find, find then she past out after that. Sirus look at her then picked her up and took her outside where the paramedics surrounded them. Alexander had his back turned then turned around when Kerry gasp and pointed at Kim who was being taken to the ambulance by the stretcher, he stomp over to her but stop when he saw Sirus touch her check then kiss her head in an affectionate way. Alex clench his teeth then tighten his fist and walk over to them pushing Sirus out the way he ask the medics to let him go with them.

When they agreed he turn to Sirus and glared at him, if looks could kill he would be six feet under making his way to hell for permanent residence. Sirus only raise an eyebrow at him and turned around walking away. Alex held Kim's hand as they were transported to the hospital, his father followed to ease Kerry's mind. As they sat in the hospital the doctor came out and told them that Kim has a concussion and has to be kept to make sure she remains in good condition.

Kim why the hell didn't you get out of the building when you heard the alarm, Alex ask as soon as he walked into her room. She sat up and told him everything that happen causing him to move his hands through his hair in a frustrated manner. So they have the recent files the company lost ask Charles, Kim shook her head no and told them that she found it a bit suspicious that the man laptop did not have the company logo and also that her expertise is in software engineering not network engineering so why come to her, how did he know she was in the break room so she played it smart and send the files to the computer at home deleting all trace on his laptop, he practically got a blank computer she said.

That's my girl Alex said while getting up to kiss her, I will be back stay in bed doctors order he said with pointing with a serious face. Resting her head back on the bed she was thinking when she heard the door open and close and kept her eyes closed. Feeling hands on her face a kiss went on her lips but it did not feel like Alex lips, opening her eyes she was meant with Camron face making her push him away quickly and scream.

Camron what are you doing? Why did you do this? she rush out, Kim Camron said breathlessly, I am in love with you, Alex do not deserve you like I do, please come with me. He inch closer to kiss her again but she push him away telling her she does not feel that way about him, she is in live with Alex. Camron became so upset he started trashing the room then got on top of her chocking her, I cannot stand people like Alex and Sirus they take everything, use people then throw them away like garbage, he use his other hand and rip the hospital gown she was in, I will not lose to them, I will be your first he finish saying while unbuckling his pants.

Kim tried to get air back in her lungs to scream when he had let her go but it was hard, pinning her down he pulled down her underwear, that is when Kim found the courage to scream only to had a hand place over her mouth. I am connecting us and as he was about to enter he was thrown off by Sirus who punch him to the ground, he went over to Kim only to be turn around and knock unconscious. Sirus Kim sobbed, now where were we Camron said darkly causing her to push the button, she was so distracted that she didn't see Camron had gotten close enough to grab her leg and pull her to him.

As she was about to enter again, Alex who walk in on the scene ran to Camron and threw him into a wall. You sick son of a bastard, how dare you touch what's mine, Alex kept punching him satisfied by the cracking of bones he heard, you tried to harm my woman your dead he said darkly and delivered the final blow to his head making him drop on the floor. He went and covered Kim only to feel something jump on his back and stab him in the shoulder. Alex flip Camron over throwing him to the ground then remove the knife from his shoulder throwing it on the ground, when Camron got up and launch at Alex, Sirus awoken to see what was happening and quickly jump up picking the knife up and launching it in Camron killing him in an instant.

Alex grab Kim wrapping his arms around her, then he looked at Sirus, is it just a coincidence that you came here to check on Kim or are you a stalker? Sirus laugh and said, I guess I got good luck when it comes to a damsel in distress.

Pulling his lips in a thin line he watch the nurses rush in but kept his eyes on Sirus curiously.

Chapter 22

As the police take statements, Alex sat on the bed next to Kim watching everyone work. Sirus who had just finish talking to the police walked over to them, I am so sorry about Camron, he should have never been here in the first place but when he realize he was close to saying something secretive he shut up. Alex squeeze his eyes together looking at Sirus, Kim lean forward touching his hand, I want to thank you for everything and I forgive you.

Sirus nodded with a smile then turn around and left, the doctor check up on Kim and said she can leave. After getting up they made to the car, tell me you are not really considering being friends with Sirus again Alex ask while his eyes are on the road. Kim huff and said, forgive him yes, be friends with him no, I know what you are thinking that I am trusting him but I do not at all trust him, he broke it and with me trust is hard to come back.

Alex grab Kim's hand and kiss it, do me another favor he pause then continued, keep your distance from Sirus, there is something more about him but I cannot put my finger on it. Kim unbuckle her seat belt, leaning forward she kiss Alex on the cheek, I promise I will keep my distance from him after all he was the one who cause us to be separated.

When they arrive home Alex made his way to the home office where he discovered his father, Brandon and Jarod waiting for him. We need to talk about what happen, it is possible somebody is targeting Kimberley as well as the company and I have a feeling Sirus showing up is not a coincidence. I am going to talk to Sirus father next week after the banquet because your mother postponed it to many times and she will kill me if we have to do it again. Alex nodded at him then spoke, well we can't wait for next week lets have Mike and Frank dig deeper for anything on Sirus and whiles they are at it, check up on Mr. Valentino.

As Kim was walking she listen to David talk about his day and came to a stop looking at the portrait that sat on the wall. She realize that the picture was her handy work then a flashback came to her of what her father said on the recording, you will find the software disk by the painting that captures the happiest moment in our life. She lift the portrait off the wall and turn it over then proceeded to search for anything indicating that it can lift up.

A gasp escape her lips because she found it, pulling out a disk she felt joy knowing that her father's work is in her hands, she ran to Alex office with David on her heel. Alex you would not believe what I have found she said holding up the disk, what is that Charles ask smiling at Kim, it is the software my father left his last clue was about the portrait he gave you, it was a portrait I painted when I was young before mother's passing.

Alex got up and went closer to her, am happy you found it, now what should we do with it. Kim looked at the disk then to Alex. She then looked around the whole room, I don't know what to do with this, it will only cause us trouble in the future. Alex stare at her for a second before grabbing the disk and placing it between a book on the shelf, for now lets keep it safe we do not want to get rid of your father's work just yet.

Oh there you are come on the banquet is two days from now and I want you to look your best, lets get going Kerry said pulling Kim by the arm. Son what are you thinking Charles spoke after they left, Alex walk over to where he place the disk and take it out. I am going to let somebody else take a look at this without Kim's knowledge the less she knows the less danger she is in. Walking out of the office he got on the phone, Jarod I need your special team of computer geeks there is something I want them to work on in secret.

The mall was more crowded today than usual but that did not stop Kerry from dragging Kim to every store to find the perfect dress. As they look around a royal blue dress captures Kim's eyes, that's the one Kerry said behind her, Kim looked around and smile at her, it sure is she replied. Paying for it they left to find something to eat before heading home, Kim could not shake off the feeling that she was being watch, is everything okay Kim she heard Kerry ask with concern, smiling she said yes it's just my mind playing tricks on me but deep down she knew it was more.

When the arrive at home, Kim made her way to her room and sat on the bed, hearing a knock she told the person to come in and was grace with Alex presence. You look tired he said then laugh, my mother have a way of doing that to the women she sees as her daughters, Kim laugh then hold her arms open for him to come to her. As he wrap his arms around he they pull apart then shared a passionate kiss, it was slow and sweet, would you like to stay with me tonight Kim ask as Alex trail kisses down her neck, he moan a yes before pulling himself and her together as they lay in bed.

Meanwhile a car approach a man standing in the dark on the bridge, you had one job but you blew it, first off you let that idiot Neil mess up everything luckily I got rid of him and his son Stephen so they won't get in our way, second Camron was suppose to die before he tried to get to Kim, not only the police are going to figure out that he take drugs that had just hit the streets, I do not trust you we might be family but you was not raise by me. The man who arrive in the car laugh, I don't care at least you got rid of those two less work for me but I am not letting you come between me and my plans.

What plans is that? the man on the bridge ask, you think you were the first one to fall in love with Kim he pause then said no. While she was taking care of you I was admiring her for being an incredible girl, even when I was send to Australia for boarding school it was horrible until she came to me selling girl scout cookies she offered to sit and talk to me and then help me make friends because her cuteness draws people in and she was right.

So you see she was practically my girl but when her father figured out who I was I tried to explain that she was way to young for me and I saw her as a sister but he saw through my act and kept her away from me, he knew who I was from his research so I had to make up a plan to get rid of him so I ask Stephen to dig and found out about his software knowing that you wanted something from Edward Jones after investing in his projects.

In the end you were just my pawn Mr. Valentino and now I can get rid of you and take my rightful place to what I so much deserve. A shot rang and the man in the car step out to Mr. Valentino who was on the bridge. Looks like your reign is over with that the man shot Mr. Valentino who died slowly.

CHAPTER 23

Okay so the cooks, servers, musicians, guest list and decorations have been check and it looks like everything is in place any other thing or things I forgot Melissa, Kerry ask looking up from the tablet she was holding. In a sarcastic tone Melissa said, Yeah a professional planner so we don't have to work so hard and in return Kerry smack her on the arm. Melissa you and I both know it is the women of the Diaz duty to throw a Banquet, it is to show people that we are capable of showing our place and elegancy in this family.

Am sorry but isn't a Banquet for people to collect their own food why do you need servers asked Kim. Grabbing her Kerry said because we don't want people to start thinking that we have no money, they will start thinking we had them serve themselves because we could not afford servers, darling this banquet is different from the ones you had in school or wherever. Kim smile at her then squeak when Kerry pulled her along, now lets go get you a dress that will have my son drooling and tripping over his feet all night when he look at you.

After a half an hour they reach the dress shop, well here we are my favorite place Kerry said with excitement. Wow that is something Kim spoke with confusion, you do know this is a bridal shop she continued. Kerry laugh, yes but I have a secret weapon to get the most beautiful dresses a lady could have, yea and you might never know when you will have to come back her for a wedding dress Melissa said who was trailing behind them.

Making their way in the shop Kerry made her way to the back for a few minutes then came out with a lady with red hair, a red dress, and red shows. Melissa whispered into Kim's ear, That's Amber but we call her Red because all she wears is red, you would think she is the descendant of little red riding hood, when I first saw her and she gave me attitude I ask where is the wolf when you need one. Kim giggle and told Melissa that was rude but Melissa just shrug and said well she was rude to me.

Hi my name is Amber, Kerry told me you need a dress that will knock Alexander off his feet, well am your girl she rushed out then grab Kim's hand pulling her to the back for fitting. Now what color do you think will look amazing on you, no wait I am seeing you in a royal blue dress so lets get to work she said excited. After a while Kim was done with her measurements and picking of patterns, she made her way to the front where Kerry was on the phone telling Alexander to calm down and that Kim was with her.

Melissa walk over to Kim, that dude need to seriously relax, he is about to give himself high blood pressure at a young age. Kim looked at Kerry, what was the purpose of buying me a dress at the mall then coming here to create one, I think you are doing to much am fine with that dress at home, Kerry said yes I know that but I was visiting a friend whose daughter bought the same dress.

She has had a crush on my Alexander since they were in Highschool but he never showed no interest in her and I feel if you and her show up in the same dress, that she devil will try to sabotage yours, she even said since she heard Alexander was seen buying a royal blue and black tux she thinks will match him and his eyes will be on her all night. I not saying that your beauty and his love for you will capture Alex eyes but I want you to be so damn hot that he will follow you everywhere and don't have time for that girl Kerry ranted.

Well since you put it that way I have an idea that will highlight that dress Amber is creating and am pretty sure I will have to thank evie from descendants for this inspiration Kim said while smiling. They continued to shop and set things up for the banquet, Kerry found David a nice little tux for him to wear at the banquet. I have to use the bathroom can you wait here for a few minutes Kim ask causing Melissa to roll her eyes, girl go where do we have to go right now our food isn't even ready yet, Kim thank them then ran off to the bathroom where she met a women looking in the mirror.

After she finish relieving herself Kim walk out of the stall to find the women still looking in the mirror. Excuse me are you alright miss she ask, the women smile and said am fine Kimberley. Kim gasp at he women and started stepping back slowly, she didn't know who this women was to know her name. Don't be afraid child, I am here to warn you be careful at the Banquet and make sure you stay by Alexander or his family side all night.

Who are you Kim ask but the women cut her off saying who I am is of no importance, but my mission is, I made a deal along time ago to a close friend that I will protect her family when she pass and when she did and left her family to the dogs knowing it will be theres and the Diaz family downfall. Now am paying for that sin because I have lost people and what hurt the most is it could have been prevented if I had just open my mouth and stop my jealousy for that person.

Who was that person? Hearing that question the women looked up at Kim and said that person was her the only thing she had that cared for her. She walk up to Kim and handed her a bracelet, this is a gift that will help you in your time of need wear it at the banquet and when you are in a situation that needs assistance squeeze it tightly. Kim smile at the woman then left making her way to Melissa and Kerry she place the bracelet in her bag. Thinking of the women she felt preparing for the Banquet is tiresome and crazy.

CHAPTER 24

harles, Brandon, Alexander, Mike and Frank made their way to find Mr. Beckford, Sirus father who is living far away from civilization. They had left early in the morning making sure that they arrive their no later that midday. As they were in the car, Charles decided to ask Alex about what his future plans are for Kim and him. Alex smile then dug down in his pocket, pulling out a box he open it and showed his father the ring.

Holy crap I knew he is whipped now he is going to be tied down for life to Kim. Alex laugh at Brandon words, I am in love with Kim and I can not see myself or her with anyone else, she is strong, independant, caring amonst other things and I will spend my life loving and protecting her no matter what comes our way.

Alex look up at his father to see him in tears, that is what it was like when I met your mother, son Kim is a great girl knowing that she came from good people she will make a great wife and great addition to the Diaz family. Alex smile at his father's words then look at Brandon who was fake crying saying how beautiful this moment is, he roll his eyes then turn to frank who told them they reach their destination.

Knocking on the door they found theirself face to face with Mr. Beckford, Charles he cough out, what brings you by to my place. Charles smile and said we are here to talk to you about Sirus. Mr. Beckford made a face of disgust at his son name then look away, listen I do not want nothing to do with that boy so whatever is the issue take it up with him, if it wasn't for his pass activities I would have left everything I own to Edward Jones and his family but don't worry when I pass away, everything I own will go to Edward and his family.

I don't understand Mr. Beckford are you trying to say you and your son have bad blood Mike ask. Mr. Edward look side to side then ask them to come in where he led them to the couch. He made his way to the kitchen and return with glasses and a pitcher of lemonade, he is starting to pour but Charles who watch his hands shake while poring take over and help him. Well where do I start ask Mr. Beckford who lean back in the chair, how about from the time you and your son start having bad blood.

Mr. Beckford laugh, we started having bad blood because that boy is not my son he is the result of my wife affair. The room went silent and Charles, Alexander, Mike, Frank, and Brandon had faces of pure shock. Who is Sirus father? Charles ask him turning his head to the side, after a few seconds Mr. Beckford replied a man associated with the mafia that goes by the name Mr. Valentino.

Alex jump up from his seat walking back and forward, I knew it that bastard was playing Kim from the beginning, he was messing with her the whole time and now he is making himself look like an angel when he probably set up Camron to hurt her. Camron that is his bestfriend he meant in England, what's going on who is Kim? Mr. Beckford ask with curiosity. She is Mr. Jones daughter Charles answered and in return Mr. Beckford suck in his breath then look at Alex, please keep that boy away from her, like I said when I die everything I have left will go to the Edward's family.

Mr. Edward is dead does it still count Brandon ask him and in return he ask how did he pass. He was murdered by Sirus biological father Charles said throw gritted teeth, then yes it does count Kim and if she has any other siblings they will have both inherit what Edward and I left for them said Mr. Beckford. Look he said looking at Alex, I can see your in love with this Kim girl so make sure to keep that bastard faraway from her, where is she from? Mr. Beckford ask.

She is from Australia Alex answered, Mr. Beckford muttered curse words from under his breath. I heard that he was obssess with a girl from that country and now I know his bastard of a father had the same obssesion with her, she was thirteen when the father started his obssesion this girl was a…but before he can finish Alex input a volunteer at the hospital and she brought him to the hospital when he was shot.

That's her Mr. Beckford answered, he got up and walk to the cabinet and pull out a folder, take this and do not look at it until after your anually banquet, gave Charles the folder. I wish that many years ago I never backstab you Charles, no one had my back like you did and I wish that I did not listen to my father nor the people I use to call my friends. Charles tap im on the shoulder then brought him into a hug, we might have outr differences but that didn't mean I wasn't going to help you, all you had to do was ask.

Mr. Beckford cried onto Charles shoulder, it felt good to be hug by someone that felt like a brother. He let go and went back to the Cabinet and pulled out a key attach to an envelope take this and open it at the banquet, I wish many years ago I gave this to you, you are the only one that care for me, I heard that you had a check sent to me when I was in the hospital, Thank you please take care and love your family with all your heart.

After spending time with Mr. Beckford they left and headed home, it was hours later from his encounter with Charles them. Hearing noise Mr. Beckford made his way downstairs where he found Sirus digging through his Cabinets, where is it old man Sirus said with venom. Mr. Beckford smiled and said it's over Sirus the truth about you is out, Sirus became so angry he charge at Mr. Beckford and stab him in the heart, you shouldn't have done that now I have to speed up my plans. Mr. Beckford drop to the floor and the life drain from his eyes and his breath stop indicating he was dead.

Chapter 25

The Banquet Ball is in full swing as everyone started to arrive, keeping the Diaz family hired helpers on their toes. Kimberley is getting dress with Melissa and as they were talking she could not shake the feeling that something else was about to happen that she would not like. Turning to Melissa, do you think I should go down there or stay coop up in my room so that if danger is lurking around I would be safe and...

Don't you dare, Melissa said with a glare, do you know how long we have been waiting for this Banquet Ball to happen. Besides, you don't want Kerry and Charles to cancel it again because they will feel sorry and want to protect you. Kimberley huff and said exhaustedly, okay, alright, I will attend just stop making me feel worst than I am.

Smiling with satisfaction, Melissa left Kim to finish getting ready. Hearing a knock, Kim told whoever it was to come in. Opening the door, Alexander stand their in all his Adonis glory, looking like the fine specimen that he is. You look beautiful he said huskily to Kim making her blush, and you don't look bad yourself, she said still red. He was up to her placing his hand on her hip and the other on her cheek, then pull her close to him and attack her lips.

Minutes has past before she pulled away, if we keep this up, we will never make it downstairs, Kim said as she is red as a tomato. Now that doesn't sound like a bad idea, keeping you locked up here away from danger, in my arms while I ravish you until the morning. Kim look like a bell pepper by the time Alexander finish talking, wow, you really don't have a filter on your mouth do you? she stuttered asking.

He looked off then back at Kim, smirking he said, when am around you, no, I love talking dirty to you because you are mine and when the night is over am going to show you that. Now lets meet our guess and no matter how insane tonight gets, please stay by my side and don't talk to anyone you do not feel comfortable with. Nodding at Alexander words she take his arm that he handed to her and together they walk downstairs.

Greeting and meeting people while she made sure to stay under Alex has Kim trying to catch a break. So this explain the reason she is sitting in the pantry, eating and breathing hard. A cook open the door only to see Kim's position, Kim smile at him, what would you like to get? she ask the man and when he reply, she retrieve his item for his dish leaving Kim behind with a chuckle.

Boss isn't going to be to happy with this, are you sure about this? Kim heard voices speaking so she lean forward. Yes I think but he said make sure, no one suspects we are here as spies, the other man said. Boss said make sure the girl do not drink anything tonight because he needs her conscience when we take her, i think for the soul propose that he like the fight she puts up.

Alright, just make sure not to be dumb and get caught by a Diaz, they show no mercy when it comes up to the people they love getting hurt. Something made noise in the background causing the men to snap their heads to the closet door where the cleaning supplies. Who is there? one of the men ask whiles the other yank open the door pulling out a maid who is crying.

Have your mother ever told you not to spy on people, the man ask in a baby voice. She shook her head vigourously then pleaded saying she would not tell no one, but it was to late because her neck is slit. Kim covered her mouth to stop her from screaming. She had prayed none of them heard her, tears started falling while she prayed for a miracle of Alexander to show up.

What do we do with the body, one of the men say pointing. Get rid of it and made sure no one see's you. When they left, Kim bolted out to the Banquet Ball only to be meant with people laying on the floor unconscious. She made her way through the house to find anyone but is meant with a crew coming with black face mask that resemble horse. Oh my gosh, Kim whispered then ran to the room David was in.

When she realize David wasn't there she turned around to leave but one of the men in black mask was shutting the door with his elbow because in his hand held a knife to David's throat. Kim broke down crying, who are you? she ask hiccuping, the man pull David with him closer to her. I am a friend of a friend who has offered a good amount of money to get you and your brother, I just didn't think you will finally be alone because Alex has a leash on you the man spat.

Please I will come with you if you leave my little brother out of this, Kim sounded heartbroken but she did not care at the moment. Her brother was in danger, the man place the knife tip on his head, you know what it sounds like a good idea, but we need to make sure we have leverage over you and your little brother here is our only option. Kim hollered but comply for the sake of keeping her brother safe.

When they pass the unconscious bodies, Kim looked around, please tell me they are not dead? she ask with a shaky voice. The man laugh then reply no, they are under a drug that is place in their drinks, they should wake up soon, so no need to worry. As they made their way to the entrance, a car was waiting for them, David got in first but when Kimberley is about to jump in, the sound of gunshots fill the air.

The car pulled off with David inside it and the man held onto Kim with a knife at her throat. The others were dead so he had nothing to loose, Mike and Frank appeared holding their guns. Let her go, an angry person bark, looking up Alexander was standing their holding a gun too, his father as well had a gun in his hand. The man looked around to see he was surrounded but did not care, he try to drag Kim to across the lawn but later his screams of pain and him dropping to the ground is heard.

What the hell Charles muttered then turn around only to see his wife holding a gun, nobody messes with my Banquet that I plan so hard on, nobody messes with my home but most important nobody messes with my girl Kimmy. Kerry has shot the man in his leg, happy she grab Kim up and headed back to the house. Remind me to never miss another Banquet because mom is packing and crazy, Alexander said with fear causing everyone to laugh and make their way inside.

CHAPTER 26

Crying and pacing the living room floor was all Kimberley can do, her little brother had just been kidnapped by vicious people. She could not help but think of the things they are doing to him, especially since they have no heart. Alexander tried to calm Kim's nerves but every time she would just cry and mumble under her breath about what can be happening to her brother.

Mike, Frank, Jarod and four unknown faces walk into the room, we have information that you guys need to hear, said Jarod. Kimberley was led to the couch by Alexander who rub her back while whispering soothing words to her. Charles nodded at Jarod to talk and so he began, It all started nineteen years ago when Sirus mother and father brought him to meet Edward Jones, they eventually mended old wounds and turn friends until Edward's wife had become ill.

She was in the Hospital for two days and during that time they both discovered she had been poison and it was affecting her unborn child. Elizabeth and Edward decided to buy a house where they would have privacy and she can try to recover but one night she pass out walking downstairs to the kitchen, this send her into premature labor.

Kim was born two months before her time and was left fighting for her life, during this time Sirus mother showed up with him following. She made a proposition to Elizabeth that if she get Edward, her husband to give up his business and turn over the software then her family will not suffer the consequences. Reports from the doctors said that Elizabeth was heard yelling at Sirus mother to get out and never return.

When Edward arrived to her room, she told him everything, but he wasn't surprise at her news, he knew what Vivian was concocting, so he sent information that he uncovered to Sirus dad. Mr. Beckford received it on a business trip to Australia and that is when Sirus family was split apart. It turns out the information consist of Sirus biological father, which clearly states that he was not a Beckford and that Mr. Beckford wife was visiting Sirus biological father every three months.

Mr. Beckford had file for a divorce and threaten to make her life a living hell, after that they argued almost everyday until one day his wife and son disappeared. Twelve years had passed, then suddenly Sirus showed up at his doorstep telling him that his mother passed away and that he had nowhere to go. At the time Mr. Beckford thought Sirus was clueless about what went down between him and his mother years ago.

But he found out he was wrong when Mr. Jones contacted him telling him not to trust Sirus and that they needed to meet. They both meant at a club in Los Angeles, where Mr. Jones told him about what Sirus and his mother had done to his wife, they hired maids to continue poisoning her causing the second child to become ill, this made Mr. Jones send his wife and second child to a vacant house far from civilization and they were safe until one night his wife was found dead in an Alleyway.

Kim could not believe her ears, so she voice her thoughts, are you sure? my father said she was sick and… but she pause thinking how her father broke the news of her mother's death to her, that's when she knew he sugar coating it for her so she wouldn't have to know the truth. Oh my God, she chock with tears falling. Kerry who had her hand over her mouth in disbelief stand up and embrace Kim, she felt her pain and this is the only thing she could do to comfort her.

Jarod continue even though he could see everyone in the room has already become poise and their expressions said they wanted to know more. After Elizabeth death, Edward threw himself into work and since Kim was old enough to take care of herself and her brother, he hired extra hands to help him, that's where Stephen comes in. He would give information to Mr. Valentino about the things Edward was working on, that is when he discovered the software.

There is just one problem, the software isn't really a software. There was never a software, everything was just a hoax to throw everyone off Edward back and Stephen knew this. The software is actually a blacklist of names of the most powerful people and their accounts of illegal doings. Sirus and his mother Vivian is on that list including Mr. Valentino but the craziest thing ever, is that Mr. Valentino was clueless about the blacklist.

Neil and Sirus with the help of Stephen tried to steal the blacklist but Edward found out and fired Stephen. Stephen also stole money from Mr. Valentino telling him that it was being invested into Edward's project. He realize that Mr. Valentino was close to finding out the truth about his lies so he had his father Neil and his Sirus hire hitman to kill Mr. Valentino.

He use the money to help Sirus when his company lost money and went to Mr. Valentine with a story that will leave a target on Mr. Edward back. When Neil contacted Sirus, he had no choice but to help because of the generous amount of money Stephen gave him. When Mr. Valentino was hit by a bullet, Kimberley who was thirteen at the time found him in an Alleyway bleeding to death and tool him to the hospital she volunteered at.

Sirus who made sure that the job was done found out about Mr. Valentino being alive and paid him a visit to finish the job but was stopped by a Kimberley when she went to check on

Valentino. This is when he meant Edward's daughter and the girl who is inheriting Mr. Beckford's will. A week later he made his way to his father Mr. Beckford angry because he could not believe that his father would give his inheritance away to a child but Mr. Beckford did not change his mind and left the will like how it was.

The will states that the wealth will be split between Kimberley and David. If Kim where to get pregnant, married or turn 21 she will receive her full inheritance and when David turn 16 he will get a partial of the inheritance and at 21 the full inheritance. This is why Neil and Sirus tried to manipulate Kim but when Kim outsmarted them making Sirus company loose everything, he made a plan to have Neil kidnap her. That whole night was stage except for Hillary being killed.

So your saying if they keep David when he turn sixteen they will be able to get half the inheritance, Mike said. That explains it, they need both Kimberley and David for the money and they need the blacklist because something like that can cause a lot on the market, Frank input. This means if we don't find David they would go to great lengths said Charles, we need to find them before they can use him to get to him.

Chapter 27

Kim could not sleep because of the thoughts running through her head. She had nightmares about what was happening to David making her get up to drink a glass of milk. Can't sleep? she heard Alex asked. Turning around she nodded and tears started to swell in her eyes. I just can't help but think that at this moment, they are hurting him, I know I might be exaggerating but... pausing she look off then hang her head down.

Shuffling was heard and a finger was place on her chin, lifting her head up Alex eyes met hers. I promise that we will find David and make sure Sirus, Neil and Stephen never see the daylight. Smiling Kim nodded but the smile did not reach her eyes. Come to bed with me, Alex said causing Kim to drop to the floor. Are you alright he ask holding unto her, yes she reply, my legs just got weak from what you just said.

I don't mean in the way you were thinking he said turning red, I mean you will sleep better with me at your side and I think I will sleep better without worrying that someone is in the house trying to take you away from me. Biting her bottom lip she followed him all the way up to his room, are you sure that I this is okay, it looks like you were working and I do not want be a burden, she said because of the junk of papers on his bed.

Alex look at her then at the bed, walking over to it he gather everything off of it and throw it on the chair, then he lift Kim up and rest her on the bed. Alex, Kimberley groan earning a smirk from him, you didn't hear me when I say you are mine and that means that no matter where I am or what am doing you will always come first. Kim look him in the eyes then her eyes glance at his lips, they keep inching closer to each other until they share a passionate kiss.

Pulling apart they try to catch their breath, Kim was staring at the floor blushing hard, she could not looking at Alex. Tilting her head up with his pointing finger, Alex wipe her bottom lip with his thumb, I promise you Kim that as of tonight you will be my love, the woman I want to wake up beside and the woman I want bare my children. We will find David and we will get Justice for your parents. Thank you Alex, Kim said in tears, laying down she felt the bed dip and arms wrap around her. Falling asleep she hears Alex whispering soothing words in her ears, with that she fell asleep.

Waking up, Kim turn over to find the side Alex slept on empty. She was starting to think last night was a dream until she look on the pillow and saw a neatly folded letter. It reads,

Good morning my love, I got a call from Mike and Frank about information on Sirus, Neil and Stephen whereabouts. Please do not leave the mansion because we believe that they are waiting to get you alone. I will be back by dinner so feel free to ask the chef to whip something up for you.

Love Alex,

Your future Husband, wink

Kim started laughing she thought his note was so sweet, this made her day a little better. Getting up she made her way downstairs and kindly ask the cooks to make her a berry pancake, the cooks were happy to oblige. She did not want to get in their way so she headed to the back yard. Looking ahead of her, Kim went out in a daze, she could not help that her mind keep wondering if David was okay or if they are feeding him. As her mind kept wondering, she heard noise from the inside of the house.

Getting up she runs to the door but stop when she hears gunshots. Not thinking twice she opens the door and the scene in front of her is gruesome, blood was everywhere and familiar faces of the staff bodies was laying on the ground, unmoving. Taking deep breaths she quietly sneak upstairs and find an empty room to hide, when she finally find one, she locks the door and picks up the telephone where she dialed Alex.

Meanwhile, Alex and his father along with his brothers, Jarod, Brandon, Mike, Frank, and a few people they hired sat down discussing the whereabouts of Sirus, Neil and Stephen. They already know Sirus kill Mr. Beckford and now that the old man is dead, the inheritance automatically goes to Kim and David as stated in his will.

So what you are telling me is that bastard is off the grid? Alex ask through clench teeth. That's correct, Jarod replies, Kim clean him out after he use her to bring the company down with the help of Melissa, he was not expecting Kim to set up meetings with the clients he stole from us to tell them about Sirus scam nor her hacking his computer to take back the money he stole from us. That day when we had to evacuate the building, that was Stephen hiring someone to get into the network but thanks to Kim quick thing she backup everything and lock them out.

The room is silent until Alex phone went off, taking his phone out of his pocket he saw Kim's number flash on the screen, smiling to himself he answer but the smile left when he heard Kim sobbing. Alex, someone's in the house and there is blood everywhere. Hearing those words Alex shouted at Mike and Frank to have their men go the house immediately. Where are you hiding Kim? Alex ask softly and she replies in the closet.

As Alex reassures her that help is on the way and she is going to be alright, banging noise is heard on the line. Kim what is that? Alex ask in a panic tone. Kim's voice went down to whisper, someone is in the room. Charles motion for Alex to put what is happening on speaker phone, as he did, the sound of Kim screaming cause everyone to flinch. Kim! Alex yelled but the line went silent.

Minutes later, deep breathing was heard before a familiar and sinister voice said, Hello Alex, did you get to say goodbye to you beautiful girlfriend before we head home because after today you will never see her again. Sirus! everyone in the room says with venom, Sirus started laughing an evil laugh, I will make sure send you an invitation to our wedding, see you when I see you, with that he hang up. Alex has gotten so angry that he started smashing things that was on his desk, breathing hard Alex spit out, the search for Sirus, Neil and Stephen is important, we must find them.

CHAPTER 28

T alking can be heard in the background as Kimberley is gaining consciousness. Opening her eyes she realizes that she is in a room that have no windows but it is decorated for a girl. Pink with a trim of white is all over, sitting up she tries to get up but notices something is heavy on her leg. Looking down she notice a lock with a chain attach to it, a snob escape her lips causing her to quickly put her hand over her mouth.

The lock on the door click indicating that someone was coming in, Kim lay on the bed covering her body with the blanket. She kept her hand over her mouth making sure she didn't make a sound. As the door open, her eyes are close tightly until the cover is remove from her and she is lift up from her position. Honey, you can open your eyes, for day after tomorrow, this face will be the only face you are going to see.

She gasp then with cold eyes she look at the man who is holding her. Sirus held her to his naked chest that is slightly muscular but not as muscular as her man, Alex. She started to think about Alexander to take her mind off the position she is in, Sirus who could read facial expressions know her attention is on that brat Alex, so he throws her on the bed and takes off his belt. I know you are thinking about that bastard and I will not allow him to take you away from me, I have work too hard for the inheritance I was suppose to get from Mr. Beckford.

That's not the only reason why I want you, believe it or not I have took a liking to you from the day we meant, it was at the coffee shop next to you High School. My mission at first was to kidnap you then keep you until you turn seventeen, old enough to bare a child but that seem day I lost my wallet and could not pay for anything. You saw me and offered me a hot cup of coffee, then you bought me a bowl of soup and gave me extract cash to catch a taxi to my destination. That day I found you to be my soul mate and when I saw you in the hospital again with my father volunteering, I knew you were my Angel.

This is why I can't have Alex take you away from me, with that he brings the belt down on her back. Her cries fill the room along with the sounds of the belt hitting her skin, after fifteen lashes he got up and left the room. The door reopen and in walks a maid, oh honey you should not upset your fiancé, he doesn't want to do it but he says it is to keep you discipline. Kim scoff, he will never get my respect, if that is what he wants tell him to go bang his mother.

I might have done nothing but bad things in my life, but I can assure you that incest is not my cup of tea, a voice said from the door. Kim froze then look at the door to see a person she thought was dead, Vivian. Impossible! Kim whisper earning a smirk from Vivian, not impossible my child, I will tell you the story of how am still alive but first tomorrow is your weding and also the night Sirus will plant his seed inside of you, in other words you will bear my grandchildren and I have to make sure you prepare.

Vivian turn around and called out for some ladies, six women fill the room, some in scrubs while others is in what seh call proper attire. Turning around Vivian look at the fearful face of Kim, the she walk to her slowly, lets begin my child. N-no, Kim stuttered sofly, stay away from me, please she beg, that only cause Vivian to take action. They strip her and tie her to the bed as tight as possible, Kim scream, cry, and call Alex name as they got to work. As I said Kimberley you are my son property now, so relax and let th women do the work, Vivian said smoothly.

Sirus and Neil were downstairs talking about what will happen once the vows are exchange. Smiling to himself Sirus turn to Neil, you know I never forgive you from you many years ago when you kill my mother. Neil smile before he said, that is why my little brother, I am doing everything to make it up to you. Sirus nodded before looking at the book shelf he did not see Neil quiertly grab a vase ready to hit him across the head.

The sound of the vase dropping and Neil sounds of cry makes Sirus head turn back to him. My boy didn't I tell you not to trust this fool at all, he mother was sneaky, he is just like her, Vivian snickered. Well I see you haven't change, you think that by helping Kimberley you would be a hero and she will willing have mercy on you, well think again Sirus says grabbing him by the throat. I can't believe you are still alive, Sirus listen to me when I say Vivian doesn't want nothing to do with you, you are her mistake that cause her to end up broke.

Liar, Vivian hollered, Sirus eyes blacken with anger before starts beating Neil to a pulp. I thought we were brothers because Edward never show you the attention I have, I guess I was wrong, Sirus said then pull out a gun aiming it at Neil head, Neil who is kneeling spits out blood then looks up in the eyes of Sirus. You have no idea what you mother is capable of but you will see her true form, with that the gun went off killing Neil.

You made the right decision Sirus, now nothing can get in your way, you have the girl and you are close to getting your inheritance. What they did not know, is that Stephen saw the whole thing played out in front of him. He left the house with a look of vengeance in his eyes, he was going to make them pay, what Neil said is right, Vivian is using Sirus as a puppet but she has a back door agenda.

Finally arriving to a hotel, he call the person he know will love to see him six feet under. Hearing his voice answer the phone had him scared, no scratch that, it had him terrified. Stephen count to ten befoe telling Alexander everything and leaving nothing out, when he finish he waited for Alex to tell him he is a dead man, he was shock to hear Alex say he is already landing in Australia, with that he hang up and lay on the bed that felt so comfortable he fall asleep.

CHAPTER 29

It is the morning of the wedding and all Kim can do is remain motionless while the maids get her ready to walk down the Isles. "Miss please, at least put a smile on your face, you will soon be Mrs. Beckford and have a beautiful family, do not disobey him," the maid says in a soft voice.

Kim scoffs again before she looks back in the mirror and thinks to herself, "This is suppose to be me and Alex's day but Sirus just keeps taking everything away from me.

The door opens and in walks Vivian, "Oh you look wonderful, this dress belonged to me when I married Sirus Stepfather." Kim is confuse, biting her bottom lip as she wonders why she address him as Sirus Stepfather instead of his name.

Vivian smile before she holds up a finger and says, "You look gloomy and that can't happen on your wedding day, I have someone that will cheer you up."

The door reopens to reveal David who runs to her as soon as he sees her. Picking him up she sobs as she pulls him closer to her.

"I miss you sissy," David says causing Kim to cry harder and say back to him, "I miss you too DJ."

A maid pulls David from Kim in a forceful way causing her to cry harder as she hears Vivian say, "Now if you want to see David everyday in one piece, be a good little girl and go through with the wedding, then bare his child or children as he instructs you too." Nodding her head, Kim allows the maids to clean the make up that is mess up from crying and put a fake smile on her face.

As she walks down the steps, she stops at the door that is open right away. Walking down the Isle, she arrives to Sirus who is standing at the alter with a huge grin on his face. Grabbing her hands, he whispers in her ears, "You look stunning."

The priest begins by saying, "My dearly beloves, we have gathered here to celebrate the union of Mr. Sirus Beckford and Ms. Kimberley Jones, as they say the vows giving to them. Any who thinks these two should not be join together speak now or forever hold your peace."

"This is the part where we step in," a voice says at the end of the Isles making everyone heads snap to it.

Happiness, relief, and joy fills Kim's body when she sees Alex, Mike, Frank, Charles, Jarod, Brandon and Alex's bother's stand there dress like they were ready for war. David who is between a maid and Vivian quickly gets up and run as fast as his little legs can carry him to them. Charles lifts him up and tucks him to the side on his waist.

Kim tries to do the same but is pull back by Sirus who looks like he wants to commit murder.   "Let her go or you will regret it," Alex says dangerously.

"NO!" Sirus yells, "I need her, no I want her, you cannot have her, I deserve everything including that inheritance. I can kill two birds with one stone, marry Kim and get the inheritance when she bares my children."

Alex can not hold his anger in anymore and yells, "Is it because you are not a Beckford and when your father disinherit you, that made that fact twice as true so you decided that Kim is the only way you can still keep your riches?"

"Besides, you not even Vivian's child," Alex says then looks at Vivian, "Isn't that right?"

"What are you talking about?" Sirus asks with confusion then he looks at his mom, "He is lying right mother?"

"No my child I am afraid he is not," A feminine voice says behind Brandon who step aside revealing the woman who Kim met in the bathroom. The woman walks up to Sirus and Kim then continues to say, "I know your are confuse Sirus but when I met Vivian thirty years ago, I never thought she would use me as pawn to get revenge."

"I was a young professor when I met Elizabeth, she was a bright student and always was one step ahead in her courses. At the same time Vivian was a good student too but her mind was focus on dating the college rich boys, she had gotten caught up into them so much that she had fail her classes."

"I wanted her to accomplish her dreams, so I hired Edward Jones to be her tutor, that is where I was both right and wrong. Her grades improve but she became obsess with Edward, so obsess she locked Elizabeth in a closet for her final exams when she found out he was interested in her as well as she in him."

"When Edward found out he confronted her in front of the whole college student body and with that she never talk to him again. She had heard about Edward enemy Mr. Beckford and with that she set her plan into motion. They had gotten married but their was just one problem, Vivian could not get pregnant, so it wasn't a guarantee that she could keep him when he started to become interested in another woman."

"Vivian travel to Australia with Mr. Beckford because he said to her he had to make amends with an old friend, so when they arrive, she was shock to see Elizabeth and Edward married and doing well."

"She was angry so she made her way to the bar, that is when she met a homeless pregnant woman who was trying to run from Mr. Valentino. That night they struck a deal with each other, Vivian said to her if she gave up her baby to her, she will make sure that Valentino never finds her, with that Sirus became Vivian's little boy and she passed him off as Mr. Beckford's child."

"She made sure cover her tracks before Sirus was born by sleeping with Valentino so that the timeline of conception matched if push came to shove. Vivian made a lot of plans which also involve using you Sirus as a benefit."

"I tried to help Elizabeth but when Vivian found out she had blackmail and threaten me. I went against Elizabeth, this is why I decided to meet Kim in the bathroom, that bracelet she is wearing is a tracking device. It also help in finding Kim, that is how we ended up in Australia."

"That's what you mean by you were fixing a wrong," Kim says making Vivian nod in response.

]With extreme clench teeth, Sirus looks at the woman who he though was his mother, "You lying whore."

"Oh please, you had just one job but completely mess that up. Now I have to take matters into my own hands, isn't that right Reagan," Vivian says with a smile as Reagan appears holding Tiffany by her hair.

"Nice to see you again and clothe, last time Neil had you naked," she says with a chuckle.

Well first things first, Reagan says then shoots Sirus, within seconds he is on the floor dead. Kim screams and is about to run to Alex but Vivian grabs Kim by the wrist and pulls her out of the building.

Reagan drops Tiffany and heads to where Vivian is but didn't make it there because Jarod tackle her to the floor. "Get off me you piece of shit," she yells at him.

"Not until you tell me the real reason why Vivian is obsess with Kim," Jarod says to her as he applies more of his body weight.

Tiffany gets up and wobbles over to the rest of them and tells everyone, "Vivian needs the money because she owes people, dangerous people. I overheard someone telling them that the Black mamba's are expecting her soon."

The who is watching the scene unfold gasps then says, "That's the reason she had tests run on Kim's body, they were preping her to be sold to the most dangerous gang here in Australia ." Hearing the maid say that cause everyone face to pale.

They all mount up into the SUV where they makes their way to the Black mamba hideout. "Mike did you call for back up?" asks Frank who gets a nod in response.

Taking a deep breath Mike says, "Okay then we wait."

Meanwhile, Kim stands before all the black mamba men as Vivian give details about the fitness and pureness of Kim. One of the men lead her upstairs to a bedroom, when they were inside, the man says, "Change into the clothing on the bed."

As she is about to finish take off her clothes the door opens revealing Vivian who have an envelope that is full of money.

Kim know it is money because she can see some of it sticking out.

"I did not expect you to hold value but somehow you do," she says as she laughs wickedly until a knife slit her throat causing Kim to back up screaming.

"Now sweetheart, where were we?" What she assume to be the leader asks.

As backup finally reach, screams echo in the house, but not just any screams, Kim's own. Alex did not wait for an order, he bang through the door then bolts upstairs. He can hear the men he came with dealing with the gang members downstairs.

When he knock down the door the sight before his eyes cause him to see red because Kim is in nothing but a panty while a man is on top of her messing with her chest. Not thinking Alex pulls him off of her and starts beating him to a pulp.

When he feels the man go unconscious, he picks Kim up and runs to safety with her. "Alex," she sobs in his chest over and over,

"Baby we are going home," he says to her and with that he walks to the SUV placing her in the seat.

Epilogue

Months has pass since Kim and David came home after being kidnap. "Hey, do you need help?" she asks Kerry who scolds her for not relaxing.

Alex had arranged for her to see a therapist because her nightmares had gotten worst, but day by day she is healing. Sirus is dead, Neil is dead, Mr. Valentino is dead, Vivian is dead, the gang members that she was being sold to is in prison for life, Stephen is serving thirty years in prison, and Reagan is in prison as well. Who isn't dead is in prison.

Kim hears Tiffany playing with her daughter and David making her happy to see she is okay and adjusting to the Diaz family. When she makes her way to the backyard, she could not help but admire the new landscape that Kerry and Charles organized. They had gotten it fixed before she came home so that she would not relapse because this is where she was sitting as half of the staff died mercilessy by the hands of Sirus men.

Kim hand rubs over the small bump that have form in her stomach. She have not break the news that she is pregnant because the doctors says stress may lead to early miscarriage. Sitting down she hears Alex starts to sing making everyone chuckle.

"My love Kimberley Jones, I have fallen hard for you and I hope you feel the same way because no matter what, you will always be mine," Alex says as he slowly walks toward her.

Getting down on one knee, Alex reach into his pocket and pulls out a velvet box. When the box is open, Kim covers her mouth with both hands. Pulling her left hand towards him he asks, "Kimberley Jones will you marry me?"

There is a pause before Kim slips unto the floor in front of him. "Yes, yes, yes, a thousand times yes," she says as the ring is slip on her finger. They both stand up after hearing applause from the crowd around them.

"Speaking of wonderful news I have something I want to tell you all," she says while she hangs her head down and smile while rubbing her baby bump. "Am pregnant!"

Alex freeze before pulling his hand away causing Kim want to cry until he kneels down and kiss her stomach cooing at it. Then he stands up and brings his lips to Kim passionately.

"Hallelujah! I am going to be a Grandmother," Kerry screams causing everybody to clap again then congratulate Alex and Kim.

As they walks upstairs to the bedroom, Alex asks, "Is it just me or do you seem different?"

Kim pecks his lips then says, "I an extremely happy because who would have thought Running from danger would send me into a protective stranger, I am deeply in love with you Alexander Diaz, and I am all yours."

"Indeed you are Kimberley Jones," he growls before leading her upstairs to their bedroom for a night full of passionate love.

www.ingramcontent.com/pod-product-compliance
Lightning Source LLC
Chambersburg PA
CBHW071002180726
48291CB00004B/1409